Mary Finch and the Spy

S S Saywack was born in Guyana in 1955 and now lives in London, United Kingdom. He has published a number of books including the Mary Finch Mysteries, of which this book is the first, and has won a number of awards.

ALSO BY S S SAYWACK

Mary Finch and the Thief

Mary Finch and the Grey Lady

Mary Finch and the Spy

Mary Finch Endgame

Mary Finch Runaway, a prologue

Perdita, the Witch and the Toyshop

Inglestone Manor

Available as both eBooks and print books.

S S SAYWACK

Mary Finch and the Spy

A Mary Finch Mystery

"presume nothing"

Arthur Conan Doyle, The Hounds of the Baskervilles

❧ I ❧

MR RENTHAM'S PARTY

Six Months Ago

THE EXPLOSION SHOOK THE STREET. A RED-HOT FLASH OF light and a clap of thunder were quickly followed by a billowing plume of acrid black smoke. For many days afterwards, the sound would ring in Mary Finch's ears. But straight after the blast, her legs felt watery, and she sat on a wall and watched the firemen at work. By the time they finished, it was clear that the house on Greek Street—the one she just walked past—was all but destroyed.

Before long, a rather lean, ferret-faced gentleman arrived from Scotland Yard. He spent some time speaking to the firemen, carefully inspected the remains of the building from the outside—it was in too precarious a state to put a foot inside—and questioned those who witnessed the explosion. He spoke at length with a well-set fair-haired boy of perhaps eighteen. Afterwards, he turned his attention to the Doctor who had been lunching nearby and attended the casualties that day.

'Gas!' he announced soberly. 'People never learn, forgetting to turn off the gas. One spark and look what happens.'

'Not anarchists, Inspector?' the Doctor replied.

'Anarchists? Whatever gave you that idea, Dr Watson?'

'Just the recent reports in the newspapers in the past few months.'

'No, no, not them,' the Inspector said, dismissively. 'We have *them* under observation—have no fear, Doctor. No, this was just an unfortunate accident. Luckily, no one was killed and the injuries are minor.'

With that, he turned away. Mary pondered the meaning of the curious look the Doctor gave him. She fancied he doubted the policeman's explanation. The Inspector's name, she found out later, was Lestrade.

Doctor Watson quickly examined her; there were only minor scratches. Then she hurried away, conscious that her employers would miss her as she was already over-due. She was working as scullery maid for the Grimwigs at the time, although it was the Butler, Mr Boots, that Mary really worried about.

SOME WEEKS LATER, MARY READ OF YET ANOTHER explosion, this time in Kilburn. She had been ill for some time and no longer worked for the Grimwigs; in fact, she was just about to take up employment with Mrs Rose Grady in Holland Park. Her old employers turned out to be criminals; they even tried to kill her. Through a combination of luck and sound judgment, she escaped them, their assassin, Black Bob, and the clutches of a mercurial thief, Davey Tupper.

As she sat on a bench in Regent's Park reading about the explosion in one of the illustrated newspapers, she noticed that James Grimwig's magnificent house overlooking the park was boarded up. The detonation, she read, was one of a series of such disasters that plagued the capital throughout the past autumn, winter and now the spring. At first, anarchists and revolutionaries were suspected. The papers speculated that while experimenting with their bombs and fuses, they might have triggered the explosions accidentally. However, with little information to go on, the press soon relegated the cause to unfortunate accidents instead, gas becoming their principal suspect. The accumulation of coal gas married to a chance spark, the press supposed, resulted in a catastrophe. It was fortuitous that no one had been killed.

The newspaper employed the latest printing technology, enabling it to print photographs as opposed to illustrations. In several of them, Mary saw the image of the fair-haired boy she had seen in Greek Street a few weeks earlier. Even though the picture of his face in the crowd was grainy, it unmistakably bore his features. He was the one the Inspector questioned.

'Blimey, another one,' Mary said.

Rose Grady, Mary's employer, glanced up from playing cards with her ten-year-old ward, Ella Sutton, and the maid of the same age, Fortune Dubois.

'Another what?' Mrs Grady asked.

'Explosion. In East Ham this time.'

Mrs Grady squinted across to the newspaper Mary, her maid, was reading. In the fading light, the old lady, she was well past sixty, and usually wore reading glasses, could not make out the small print, but the headline was prominent enough to be seen:

Violent Blast in the East End. Police deny it was the work of Anarchists.

'What's an anarchist, Miss Mary?' Fortune asked. The maid, from the West Indies, spoke with a pleasant lilt. She fiddled with her plaits and gazed up at Mary with bright, smiling brown eyes. Unusually she was dressed in

4

a pretty blue dress, not her usual black and it immediately set her apart from the other maids. In fact, she could well have passed as one of the guests at a party they were attending, albeit a poorer cousin.

'It's a…' Mary hesitated. 'A… It's something you can look up in your dictionary when you get back home.'

'Anarchists are nasty people who want to overthrow the government, Fortune,' Mrs Grady said. 'They believe wealth should be distributed evenly. They want to abolish the state—*that is, the government*—as they believe it to be harmful and irrelevant. So, they plant bombs and blow things and people up. They are criminals.'

The four-wheeled carriage they were in stood stationary between the wide gateposts of a gravel path. It had been stopped for a while, so Mrs Grady could inspect the views on offer. The sun had just dipped, but the sky was tinged with light. Although the air was warm, the elderly lady slipped a shawl around her thin shoulders. She only recently recovered from an illness and felt a chill keenly.

Mary was grateful that her mistress was returned to good health. For a time, she worried that Mrs Grady would remain sorrowful and desolate, a victim of the terrible memories raised in her encounter with Lorna Denbie, a medium she employed. But that was now behind her and this was her first major outing since that dreadful time.

The long gravel path was flanked by two lines of

mature and gnarled plane trees, each heavy with leaves and singing with birds. Manicured lawns fell away on either side. Arrow-straight, the path led to a wide circular driveway. At the end of the driveway lay a blue-green spouting fountain, and behind that was the imposing monolith that was Dunchester Hall. The fountain, as well as the house, was cleverly lit by the novelty of electricity, Dunchester Hall being one of the few houses in the capital to be so powered. At its entrance, several lamps shone brightly.

Although its Portland stone façade lay in shadow, the sun had sunk behind the building, light burned from each of the Hall's tall gothic windows. Statues of griffins and gargoyles, lions and unicorns stood as sentinels along the high battlements, looking down on all who dared approach. The Union Jack flew lazily in the breeze at the top of the embattled tower above the entranceway, a chiming clock residing in the tower's centre. On either side of it, the Hall spread itself out magnificently, an island of solidity rising up through the surrounding lawns and fields, an unashamed proclamation of wealth and power. At both ends of the house were a gravelled area filled with carriages. It was there that an army of footmen and servants were busy dealing with those who arrived.

Mrs Grady had been invited to Dunchester Hall, to attend what was gossiped to be the event of the month, although Fairchild Rentham, the industrialist and the Hall's owner, laughably called it his *little soirée*. The great and the good would all be present. It was rumoured that the Duke of York, Prince George, and his bride, Princess Mary of Teck, were invited—society talk was still of their marriage a month ago in St James's Palace, hence the security that went above and beyond the usual. The Anarchist League of Great Britain spoke out against the cost of the wedding, so policemen patrolled the grounds and mingled amongst the multitude of staff who spilled out everywhere.

As their carriage pulled up beside the fountain, Ella and Fortune's jaws dropped in awe. Their eyes refused to settle, bouncing from one magnificently dressed, jewel-bedecked lady to another. Each tugged at the other every time someone yet more resplendent than the last passed by.

'Oh, dear me,' Mrs Grady said, also noticing the ladies. 'I do feel so plain.' She smoothed back her red hair that was flecked with grey, in a nervous, self-conscious way.

'No!' Mary said. 'You're every bit as handsome as them. Ain't she, Archie?'

Her friend, Archie Dibble, a hefty boy of sixteen, two years older than her, was perched beside the driver. He agreed to accompany Mrs Grady only after Mr Venables, her Butler, was taken poorly. Archie was in a sour mood having been made to dress like a turn-of-the-century liveried servant in a horsehair wig, gold braids, white stockings and red pantaloons.

Nevertheless, he said brightly, 'You look sparkling,' although he declared that he himself looked like a peacock. However, he was not out of place as there were many servants and coachmen similarly dressed.

'Perhaps I should not have come—' began Mrs Grady.

''Ere, none of that, now,' Mary interrupted her, sternly. 'Remember what your doctor said. You need to get out and about and enjoy yourself.'

Archie leapt down nimbly, opened the door and extended an arm towards Mrs Grady.

'Go on,' Mary said, 'you'll shine. You look like Queen Vic herself—not like now, of course, but like what she was when she got married to Bertie,' she added with a crafty wink.

The old lady smiled shyly and mouthed, 'That was a little before your time, my dear.'

Mary giggled. 'Go on, Ella, you as well.'

Mary proudly watched with Fortune as Mrs Grady walked steadily to the grand door of Dunchester Hall, Ella and Archie beside her.

'Come on,' she said to Fortune, 'let's go and help out in the kitchens. That's where the real gossip is. Don't worry. Give it twenty minutes, and Ella will come and find you.'

With that, Mary vanished into a daydream.

Lady Mary Finch descends from her carriage and walks with elegant poise to the grand entranceway of the

Mary came back to reality with a start. Away from the entrance, in a fold of the building just under one of the windows, was a tall, heavy man. His head was masterful, his steel-grey eyes deep-set and alert, but his corpulent frame looked unwieldy. Dressed as he was in a dark coat, the collars tipped with red, compared to the elegantly dressed guests in their dinner jackets and evening suits, he looked almost uncouth and remarkably out of place.

However, what drew her attention was not he so much as the smaller figure of a fair-haired man of about eighteen standing beside him. He was someone Mary had seen before—once in real life and several times in newspaper photographs.

THE CLAP OF THUNDER

MARY STRAINED to listen to what they were saying, but she was too far away to hear. It was clear, however, the two were arguing. The fair-haired man shook his fist at the tall gentleman, who reached out to place a placating hand on his shoulder. It was instantly brushed away.

At that moment, a policeman walked by. They both quickly turned inwards to face the wall and fell silent. Once the policeman passed, they began their argument again, but in harsh whispers.

They spoke for a minute more until the young man suddenly swung on his heels and stormed off towards the garden, a black look on his face.

'Well, close them,' the portly gentleman shouted after him. Wearing an exasperated look, he turned and went towards the wide entrance of the Hall, muttering to himself.

Mary looked round bewildered. Had she not seen the fair-haired man before, she would probably have ignored him. The coincidence of seeing him for the second time, though, was not lost on her—especially as the other time had been in odd circumstances. He was dressed as a liveried servant, not unlike Archie, and as such, would not have seemed out of place but for the weighty satchel he was carrying. That and the manner in which he'd spoken to the portly gentleman set him apart.

Her curiosity piqued, Mary started to follow him, only for Fortune to grab her hand.

'Where you going, Miss Mary?' the small girl asked.

'Listen, Fortune,' Mary said, 'you go to the kitchens and wait. And grab a bite to eat. I'll be a while only. Go on, off with you.'

'But…' Fortune hesitated. Mary, however, hurried away just as the clock in the tower struck the half.

The young man walked with purpose, ignoring those around him, until he met a shorter, older dark-haired man dressed as a valet in black trousers and jacket, with a white shirt. Together, they went into a small gardener's hut concealed behind tall bushes in a deserted part of the grounds. The hut was some distance from the main house.

A few minutes later, they emerged. Even in the failing light and despite the shadows of the trees, Mary could make out that the fair-haired man was trailing something behind him—a wire or cord of some sort. The older man carried a box with an odd handle. They went some thirty yards to a large plane tree, and while the young man crouched behind it, the other, nervous and agitated, watched all around them. His head flicked constantly right and left.

Several minutes passed, after which the young man arose, whispered something, and pointed towards the entrance, to the Hall under the clock. He raked his fingers through his hair and walked away, leaving the other servant to settle down, hidden behind the tree and in its shadow.

Something cold touched Mary's mind. She was troubled, and that made her anxious. She was curious to know why the men behaved so strangely. Seeing the fair-haired man walking purposefully towards the hall, she followed. He still carried the satchel, though it appeared less bulky. It was odd, each time he passed a policeman, his head dropped low.

At first, Mary considered stopping one of the constables to tell him what she'd seen, but hesitated. Perhaps her imagination was just playing tricks. Perhaps it was a coincidence and nothing more that the fair-hair man should be here. But the other time she'd seen him… her brows furrowed. She shook her head, unsure of herself and what it all meant.

The man entered the Hall through a French window and she followed not wanting to lose him. He weaved his way through the crowded ballroom and set about drawing the heavy brocade curtains across the windows at the back of the room. Picking up a tray of champagne, he walked back through the room towards a corridor beyond, completely ignoring the guests.

An odd mixture of fear and excitement tingled Mary's fingers, even as she felt her face glowing with embarrassment. She'd been so distracted by her pursuit, she'd not realised that she, a lowly maid, was wandering idly amongst the splendidly dressed guests of Fairchild Rentham. Mary smiled with apologetic humility, as if to say she had an urgent message to deliver and was looking for her mistress amongst their esteemed ranks, and hurried on.

By now, her quarry had reached a door at the far end of the corridor. He knocked. A second later, it opened and the corpulent man with whom he had spoken to earlier issued out. When the fair-haired man went in, his portly companion closed the door, advanced two paces and stopped. He planted himself, an immovable object where he stood.

He caught Mary's eye, gave a smile and lifted his champagne glass slightly. Mary blushed a vivid red and hurriedly shied away. She edged backwards, trying to get behind a pillar where she could observe unseen, when a voice cried out, 'Careful, young lady.' The warning came too late. She stumbled into an elderly gentleman, who immediately grasped her elbows to prevent her from falling.

Mary looked at him in horror.

'S-s-sorry, sir,' she stammered.

Once he steadied her, he gently released her elbows and, tilting his head sideways, spoke in a smiling, fatherly way.

'No harm done, I am sure, my dear. But it is always good to watch where one is going.'

'Yes, sir. S-s-sorry, sir,' she repeated.

'But who knows—backward walking might just become all the rage one day.' Tapping his nose, he winked playfully. 'In which case, I recommend a little more practice.'

For a second time, Mary blushed. He tipped his head in a half bow, and, still smiling walked away. Mary, hot and embarrassed, swallowed nervously.

The large man was still there. Even with her lack of experience of such functions, Mary couldn't help but think that something odd was going on. All she had seen appeared strange. It was made more so as the large man appeared to be guarding the door.

She glanced around, looking for someone to speak to, when a sudden loud voice drew her attention. A small gentleman was hurrying towards the portly man in little, almost feminine steps, and shouting energetically.

'Well, mountains do move!' he said in a spirited squeaky voice.

'Rentham!' the large man said, a wide grin cutting across his face.

Fairchild Rentham, the host of this remarkable gathering, was a man as wide as he was tall. Tall, however, he was not; he stood slightly over five feet. His thinning jet-black hair was swept back harshly across his shining head. His animated heavily whiskered face gave the impression of a friendly rabbit.

'Salter, Salter,' Rentham called out, 'look whom we have here.'

'Good Lord! We are humbled, sir.' Salter, a colonel with a stiff military bearing, came to stand beside them. He was as tall as the portly man, though considerably thinner and wore a monocle stuck in one eye. 'Am I mistaken? Surely we are not in Whitehall or the Diogenes Club?'

He and Rentham laughed, and the monocle slipped free to dangled loosely on a string by his breast.

'Quite!' the object of the colonel's mirth, said, drily,

'Salter, such visits are as rare as hen's teeth,' Rentham said. 'This calls for a celebration. Come, I have a remarkable brandy in the office, bottled, I believe, two years before Waterloo.'

In a deft move, as he began to walk to the door behind them, the large man extended his arm, threaded it through Rentham's and skilfully swung him around.

'Those, sir, are what I call remarkable,' he said loudly, using his champagne glass to point towards some paintings on the landing of the sweeping staircase. At the same moment, he took several steps towards them, bringing the Industrialist with him. The colonel followed. 'If I am not mistaken, they are Gainsboroughs. Though the last time I saw them, sir, they were hanging in the National Gallery.'

'Ah! You noticed them.' Rentham sounded surprised. The paintings' prominence, however, dominating the entrance and looking down on all who arrived, suggested design. 'I have them on loan for the occasion.' He waved his words away airily. 'The director and I are on friendly terms. Since I have considered leaving my collections to the nation come the time, he has allowed me this trifle for the gathering. Now, that brandy—'

'And am I right in saying that beside them is something more contemporary?'

'Sir, I did not think art was a subject you had knowledge of.'

'It has become… a fancy,' the gentleman said. 'Renoir, I believe.'

'Indeed! You have an eye, sir. The Impressionists: a very underrated group whose works I have started to collect.' Rentham laughed. 'Mark my words, sir, the world will grow to love them.'

'Yes, I daresay. Since you are collecting, am I to assume that the recent Stock Exchange crash in New York has not affected you?'

'I foresaw the event by several months, sir.' Rentham spoke loudly, proudly even, as if he was anxious for everyone to hear his cleverness. 'The only difficulties I experienced were in removing my capital without alerting the market to my knowledge. That I managed to do with more than a week to spare.'

'Then business is good, no doubt.'

'It will be better with the government contract we have been discussing.' Rentham gave a smile that spoke of money. 'Arms, sir! That is where wealth is these days.'

'Especially with the situation in Germany,' Colonel Salter added with a slight cough. Unconsciously, he was polishing the lens of his monocle with a handkerchief.

'Yes. Their growing navy. Quite,' the portly gentleman replied in a manner that suggested he was neither impressed nor surprised.

'Of course, we would not do business with them,' Rentham added quickly.

'Indeed,' the gentleman said in the same manner as before. 'I am glad to see we are all *good* Englishmen. And how goes the work?'

Rentham gave a tight-lipped smirk. 'Just an hour ago, we reviewed the new designs. I think the Admiralty will be pleased with the progress.'

The tower clock began the preamble chimes to mark the hour; in a few seconds it would be ten in the evening. The first strike mingled with a Mozart Concerto rising from the grand ballroom.

The portly man looked up. 'Now, sir, about that remarkable brandy you mentioned.'

'Ah! Yes. One of just three bottles remaining. Did

you know, a bottle was reputed to have been drunk by Lord Cardigan the evening *after* the charge of the Light-Brigade.'

'No doubt he needed it,' the portly gentleman joked and the others laughed.

'Another was drunk at the Queen's Golden Jubilee. So it is more than fitting for one to be drunk on this auspicious occasion—'

The explosion was like a clap of thunder.

THE HALL SHOOK VIOLENTLY. Mary's heart leapt into her mouth. She knew immediately there had been an explosion. She'd heard such a noise once before, in Greek Street. Like then, her legs wobbled.

The electric lights went out, came back on again, flickered several times before they were finally extinguished. Only the candles remained to light the rooms in dancing flickering shadows.

Howls erupted from all around. Women were screaming, men shouting, people were rushing here and there in a panic. A noisy crowd streamed out of the rooms and out of the house.

'My God! What's happened?' Rentham shouted. He rushed to push his way through the crowd towards the source of the thunder.

Mary was just about to do the same when she

stopped. Amongst the panic, she saw the portly man standing perfectly still, a silent island ignoring the hurricane raging around him. He raised the glass of champagne to his lips and drained it. Then, in the same serene manner, he deposited the empty glass on to a table beside him. A smug, almost conceited smile came to his face as he brushed some dust from the sleeve of his jacket.

Mary hurried away to the ballroom, searching for Mrs Grady and her companions. The French windows where the brocade curtains had been drawn, were blown in. They now hung limply from their fixings, draping the ground, the shattered windows behind them. They had prevented the blast from peppering the room with shards of glass, although this was not entirely the case. Several people were bleeding from minor cuts.

She picked her way through the room littered with champagne glasses, items of loose clothing, capes and scarves, shoes that the guests discarded in their hurry to get away. Neither Mrs Grady nor her companions were there. Mary went to the patio, hoping to find them outside.

It was immediately obvious, that the small gardener's hut was the site of the explosion. It was gone, demolished, and a fire was busily consuming what little remained. Several people, the police included, were rushing towards it.

To her surprise, there was the young man again. He was slipping through the panicking crowd, deftly weaving past them, going in the opposite direction to everyone else, heading for the open ground behind the Hall. He was carrying a large flat case under his arm. The other servant, the one who had been crouching behind the plane tree, joined him.

Mary's mouth gaped wide, understanding who they were. 'Bombers!' she whispered. She grabbed at a policeman. 'Them, they did it.' She pointed to the retreating men.

'Yes, yes,' he said haughtily, breaking away from her and heading towards the gardener's hut.

'It's no point going there.' Mary tried to get his attention, but he disregarded her completely.

They were getting away and her blood was up. Seeing no other option, she charged after them. They were running across the lawn to the hedges of a formal garden, which they quickly passed through. Beyond that was a screen of trees. That was the perimeter of the grounds, behind which, no doubt, were several roads leading away from Dunchester Hall.

Mary had to hurry. The half-moon gave sufficient light to show her the way, but once they reached the trees, she would lose sight of them. She ran harder, only hearing the thrumming of her heart and the rasping of her breath. The sounds from the house behind her were murmurs lost in the night.

At the very moment Mary made the trees, a dark figure stepped out, blocking her way.

'I'll take care of this,' a gravelly voice bellowed.

Mary stopped, as if suddenly frozen in a hard frost. Her mouth went dry and a sickly panic twisted her stomach into sharp, tight knots.

'Mr Boots?' she gasped. The figure stepped nearer and Mary stumbling backwards in amazement, lost her balance and clattered to the ground.

She stared up at him, the ex-Butler of the Grimwigs, her former employer, with wide disbelieving eyes, fearfully remembering the last time they met. He hovered over her. The large gruff man curled his lips nastily and his eyes narrowed and Mary flinched. His puffy, petulant face was dark with menace.

'Mary Finch,' Boots said. An odd, ominous smile creased his face. 'I thought it was you. Well, I'll be… Mary *bloody* Finch!'

Even as Boots took a step towards her, he was pushed aside by the fair-haired man.

'Finch? Mary Finch?' he said as if confused.

'Get on with you,' Boots barked at him. 'Make sure the stuff is safe. I'll take care of this.'

Instead, the man pushed Boots to one side. The next thing Mary knew, he'd grasped her wrist and dragged her up. The moon was behind him and his face was hidden in shadow, but she knew he was looking at her intently.

'What the hell's this?' he shouted. He grabbed the broken locket that Mary always wore and she felt the sharp scratch of pain as he tore it from around her neck.

'Give that back!' Mary flung her fists at him, but the dark figure didn't move. Scrutinising the broken locket, he appeared puzzled and seemed rooted to the spot. 'Give that back!' Mary pleaded again, trying to claw it from his grasp.

To her utter surprise, rather than pushing her away, he dragged her closer until they were facing each other. He was looking at her, and suddenly fearful of what he might do, Mary was about to scream when he shoved her away. A firm push propelled her through the air, arms and legs flailing, and sent her sprawling across the grass. Even as Mary landed, she saw him fling her locket towards her. She scrambled to where it landed, clutching it tightly.

'Run!' the young man shouted.

'I've got business to settle first,' Boots snarled.

'There ain't time, look behind her.' A mass of policemen was converging on them.

'She knows me. I've got to fix her first,' Boots said. But as he advanced, a charging figure crashed headlong into him and both fell back into the shadow of the trees.

'Get him off me!' Boots shouted.

To Mary's astonishment, as if ejected from a canon, Archie Dibble hurtled through the air from the trees to land with a crash beside her. Behind him came several cries of '*Run!*'

Archie quickly rose to his feet and was about to charge back into the fray when his legs buckled and he slipped down. He was bleeding from his nose and lips.

'It was Boots, Archie. I saw Mr Boots.' Mary rushed over to him. 'I was chasing his accomplice, and then there he was.'

'Boots? Mr Grimwig's butler?'

'I swear it was him.'

'What's he doing here? What's his game?'

'It's them that did the bomb.'

'That was a bomb?'

'They blew up the shed,' and Mary pointed to the fire by the bushes. Archie stared at the blaze in bewilderment, and then to where Boots and the others had gone.

'I was looking for Mrs Grady and the girls when I saw you haring away,' he explained. 'Ow!' he cried somewhat nasally as his fingers came to his nose. When he saw the blood, he cursed loudly. 'It's broken, ain't it?'

'Here's two of them.' A voice, singular in authority, came from behind them. Mary and Archie spun around. Several figures, unmistakably policemen, were converging on them; even in the darkness, their uniforms were distinctive. 'In the name of the law, remain where you are.'

'Who do you have, Gregson?' a familiar voice shouted.

'Two of the anarchists, I'll warrant, Lestrade,' said Gregson. There was unmistakable pride in his voice.

A SURPRISE

'ANARCHISTS? My left foot. I'm afraid you're mistaken,' Inspector Lestrade said in a superior tone as he drew level with Gregson. 'This one is Mary Finch. She's a maid to Mrs Grady of Holland Park. Remember the Denbie affair a few months back?'

Gregson, a tow-headed inspector in contrast to his dark-haired and shorter colleague, nodded. 'And this one?' he asked.

'Archibald Socrates Dibble,' he said with a certain irritation in his voice. 'His grandfather owns the pie shop in Baker Street.'

'The one next to Mr Holmes?'

'The same,' Archie said, somewhat nasally.

'Hurry.' Mary pointed. 'They went that way. There's three of them. Two dressed as servants and Mr Boots, an older man. They're getting away—'

'I've got this,' Gregson said. Before his companion could do anything, he was quickly off, his men following. 'Take them back, Lestrade, and find out what they know,' he shouted.

Lestrade scowled contemptuously, watching his fellow officer vanish under the trees. No doubt he'd rather be on the chase than acting as chaperone. Dr Watson once told Mary, there existed a fierce rivalry between the two Inspectors. She could see it imprinted in the policeman's face.

'We seem to meet in extraordinary circumstances, Miss Finch,' Lestrade said as they walked back towards the hall. 'I hope you're not carrying any *magical* powder.' The last time they met, Mary blew some strange dust in his face that caused him to hallucinate.

'About that, Inspector. I didn't mean—'

'Yes, I'm sure you didn't,' Lestrade said, sourly. Archie instantly regretted his mocking snigger as he clutched his aching nose. The black look the Inspector gave him made him turn away.

As they walked, Mary explained what just happened. Lestrade listened in silence, occasionally glancing over his shoulders to where Inspector Gregson went. He wore the face of a morose and disappointed man. In front of them, the hall was now quiet. The commotion had died down; the electric lights were on again; the fire where the hut had stood was extinguished. On the drive, rows of carriages were slowly making their way along, and a traffic jam was growing as the partygoers tried to hurry away.

'Well, it's a good thing Prince George didn't attend,' Lestrade said. 'An assassination attempt is the last thing we need.'

'By anarchists?' Mary glanced towards the hut with a puzzled look on her face.

'We had intelligence to that effect.' Lestrade moaned, his eyes still fixed where his colleague went. 'That Gregson is a clot; they'll easily slip through his fingers. I really should have taken up the chase.'

By now, they were crossing the paved patio by the house to an open French window. Several figures could be seen moving in the room beyond. On the patio, at the side of the window, Ella and Fortune waited. A policeman, seeing Lestrade approach, stepped out and waved the small girls away. When they wouldn't go, he turned his full attention to them.

'We're waiting for Miss Mary.' Fortune gave him a stern look.

He was about to argue when Lestrade shouted irritably, 'Leave them be, Warner, and make yourself useful. Start questioning the staff.'

'But sir—'

'Lestrade? Is that you?' It was Colonel Salter. The anger in his voice matched the rage etched into his face. 'Who are they?' He glared at Mary and Archie. 'The thieves?'

'Thieves? No, sir, witnesses to the bombing, sir,' Lestrade announced, confused.

'Bombing? What was the point of having Scotland Yard here?' he said. 'The bomb is the least of our worries.'

As he stepped into the room Rentham called his office, Lestrade gasped in horror. 'My God!' he cried. 'But-but-but—'

The room looked to having been visited by a tornado. Surrounding a large safe by the wall were the remains of many cushions. They came from the chairs that populated the office. Each cushion had been gutted, torn and charred, the feathers and stuffing that filled them scattered like confetti to every corner. There was a burnt smell in the air. It did not come from the fire that consumed the hut in the garden, but from the explosion that'd torn the door off the safe. It hung loosely from the box like a broken jaw.

An electrical wire running from the safe, across the floor and behind a solid mahogany desk, caught Mary's attention. The wire was plugged into a socket on the wall. On the desk was a small square box with a T-shaped handle sticking out from the top. Mary recognised it as the one she had seen carried to the tree near the gardener's hut.

The scene in the room was familiar. Mary read of something similar in one of her Penny Dreadfuls. As the truth dawned on her, she glanced towards the hut, and back to the safe. Her fingers twitched and began drumming against the side of her leg.

'Yes, *Inspector!*' Rentham shouted, sarcastically. 'That's right, *Inspector.* We have been robbed, *Inspector.*'

The Industrialist sat as if poleaxed, guzzling from a crystal glass filled with an amber liquid—no doubt his eighty-year-old brandy—doing so with very little relish.

'A robbery? But-but-but—' Lestrade's eyes also flicked towards where the hut had been.

'Anarchists I might expect, but this?' Rentham swallowed almost half the contents of the glass in one gulp.

'But-but-but—'

'Will you stop saying that!' Rentham screamed. 'What are you doing about this?'

'C-close the gates,' Lestrade shouted to Constable Warner. 'Q-quickly, before they all go. We need to search everyone—'

'Have you taken leave of your senses, Inspector?' Colonel Salter said, a perplexed look on his face.

'Insane! Totally insane.' Rentham threw his hands up in despair.

'We must search them, sir, before—'

'Search *my* guests?' Rentham jumped out of the chair. '*Search my guests?*' he screamed. 'Are you mad? Do you know who *my* guests are? There are Dukes and Earls and Princes. Royalty, man. My God, there are several Viscounts numbered amongst them.' He came forward menacingly and Colonel Salter grasped his arm.

'Everyone who is someone is *my* guest. Search them and their wives like they are common criminals? Have you lost your mind? This is the work of the Anarchist League of Great Britain. It is they you should be searching—every man jack of them, and *not* my guests.'

'But-but-but…' Lestrade began, looked at Rentham and quickly glanced away. 'I don't understand. Two explosions? In the garden and here? How did they manage to set off both explosions at the same time? I mean, they must have, otherwise we'd have heard two bangs and we… I only heard one.'

'The cushions?' Rentham suggested, caustically.

'No, no, sir,' Salter said in a quiet and considered tone. 'Even with them, the bang would have been loud, only a little less so. Loud enough for us to hear—after all, we were just outside the door. The Inspector is right—both explosions must have happened simultaneously.'

'While we were standing outside the room?' Rentham sank back into his chair.

'Of course. It couldn't have happened earlier,' Salter said. 'We were inside this room not thirty minutes before when we placed…' He fell silent and nodded towards the safe. 'Nothing was amiss then. This occurred after we left.'

'Under my very nose?'

'Please, sir, if I can say something—' Mary began.

'But-but… I mean, I don't understand,' Lestrade said.

'That's patently obvious,' Rentham snapped.

'Ahem! Sir, please, if I can say something—' Mary tried again.

'Two bombs? But I don't understand,' Lestrade repeated.

'So you keep reminding us.' Rentham glared at the floor.

'Please, sir,' Mary said once more.

'What was the point of having you here, Lestrade?' Rentham scowled bitterly. 'You and half of Scotland Yard!'

'Sir, please, if I can say something,' Mary raised her voice.

'And who the hell are you?' Rentham's furious gaze fixed on her. Mary glared back, equally furious.

'Mary Finch. And are you always this rude?' She gasped at her forwardness as she saw Rentham preparing to shout. 'What happened is obvious, ain't it?' She spoke quickly before he could. Rentham, taken by surprise, leant across the polished mahogany desk, supporting his weight on his hand. His rabbit face twitched crossly.

'Is… that… so?' he said, softly and slowly.

'Of course, it is,' Archie said, loudly.

Rentham, Salter and Lestrade looked at him, and Archie swallowed loudly and looked shyly towards Mary.

'Yeah,' he said in quiet and hopeful tone. 'Mary knows… don't you, Mary?'

'You found that behind a tree near the gardener's hut, didn't you?' Mary pointed at the odd box on the desk.

'You know what *that* is?' Salter asked in a superior tone.

Mary gave him a scowl. 'I might be a girl, Colonel, but I ain't stupid. It's a detonator box, innit? You push the handle down, and that sends electricity along wires to set off some explosives. Miners use them—as well as people who wants to blow up huts, apparently.' Mary gave him a snooty smile. 'And that wire,' she nodded to the one on the floor at the side of the desk, 'was used to set off the explosives on the safe. Set it up and flick the power on from the wall switch and Bob's your uncle.'

The colonel was startled. Rentham and he glanced at each other, then to the detonator box, the wire, and back to Mary.

Taking advantage of their silence, Mary continued. 'The bomb in the garden was a much bigger and louder affair. It had to be, to conceal the one that blew open the safe. And the Inspector is right in thinking the bomb in the garden must have been a diversion to cover up the noise from this one,' she added kindly.

Lestrade looked dumbly at Mary and slowly nodded his head, mumbling something inaudible that sounded a little like, 'yes, as I was going to say…'

'What makes you think that?' Salter asked Mary.

'Well, why else do it?'

'Because they are anarchists, perhaps?' the colonel mocked.

'What? An anarchist wasting good dynamite to blow up a gardener's shed when he's got half the toffs in England waltzing a couple of hundred yards away? Nah! They're robbers. The safe is what they wanted.'

'Poppycock!' Rentham blurted.

'Come on, Mister. Was anyone killed?' Rentham's glare made Mary swallow and she continued speaking quickly, but a little less loudly. 'A few minor cuts was all I saw. And did you notice that the curtains were drawn at the back of the big hall, across the windows in front of where the bomb was?' The Industrialist wore a puzzled look. 'Someone took care so as no one would get a face full of broken glass, is why. And tell me, where did everyone look when the bomb went off? Not in here. Everyone, me included, was eyeing what'd happened in the garden. We were all running around like headless chickens—coppers and all.'

'Both explosions happened exactly at the same time,' Lestrade said. 'No matter how good their stopwatches were—'

'They didn't need stopwatches,' Mary said. Lestrade shot her a cocky look. 'They had a clock instead.' Mary flicked her head towards the tower outside where the clock was. 'Both bombs went off when the chimes struck the fourth stroke at ten o'clock. One-stroke, two-stroke, three-stroke, and *bang* on the fourth,' she clapped each stroke, the last one louder than the others.

'How do you know that?' Rentham's mouth twitched, his eyes screwing up.

'Bravo! Bravo! Bravo!' The tall, rotund gentleman entering the room, was clapping. His face was bright and cheery, his steel-grey eyes twinkled mischievously. 'At least one chicken still has its head. However, it happened on the sixth chime.'

'Him!' Mary yelled and pointed. 'He's one of them. I saw him with one of the bombers. Arrest him, Mr Lestrade.'

'Are you mad?' Rentham shouted. Then, regaining his composure, he managed to say softly, 'Do you know who this is?'

'A bleeding crook, is who,' Mary said tartly, giving the rotund man a dirty look.

'Allow me to present—'

'No, no, allow me to introduce myself,' the tall man interrupted, giving a slight bow while still smiling. 'Mycroft Holmes at your service, Miss Finch. I believe you are acquainted with my brother, Sherlock.'

❦ 5 ❦

MYCROFT HOLMES

'MR HOLMES?' Mary gasped.

'Finch? Finch?' Mycroft Holmes mused. 'Ah, Finch! Yes, now I recall. The Boat Train Mystery. It was you who furnished Sherlock with the final clue, I believe, or so Dr Watson informed me.'

That happened many years ago when Mary first met the detective. As far as she was aware, only Sherlock Holmes, Dr Watson and Archie knew the story. She was not aware, however, that the great detective had a brother. That only added to her confusion. That and how remarkably different they were—Sherlock, lean and tall, to Mycroft's considerably larger and stouter frame. One energetic, the other, she thought unkindly, indolent. Only their eyes betrayed their kinship—a faraway introspective look resided in the gaze of each man. That Sherlock Holmes's brother might be involved in this affair—a common burglary—seemed unlikely. Yet she'd seen what she'd seen.

'But you were talking to the man who did this,' Mary said. 'Outside, when I first arrived. You and him were arguing.'

Mycroft Holmes pouted, seemingly recalling something, and he shook his head slowly.

'No, I am afraid not, Miss Finch. Yes, I was speaking to *someone*. That was my aide, Mr Jeremy.' He indicated to a brown-haired, middle-aged man standing just in the hallway, who returned a courteous smile.

'No, it wasn't,' Mary said. 'He looks nothing like the man I saw. For a start, he was younger with fair hair and he was—'

'Wearing livery?' Mycroft Holmes said. 'At the time, Mr Jeremy also wore a wig, not unlike the one your young friend is wearing—perhaps that is why you mistook the colour of his hair. Is that not right, Mr Jeremy?'

'I can find the items if they are required, sir,' Mr Jeremy said.

'But that's not right,' Mary said. 'Wait, I saw you let the man into this room, ten minutes before the bomb went off. He knocked and you—'

'*I?*'

'Yeah, you!'

Mycroft Holmes took a deep breath. 'Let me recall,' he said, slowly.

'Do you know slander is a crime, young lady? Do you know what you are saying?' Rentham asked. 'The very idea that this gentleman would consort with anarchists—'

'No, no, she is quite right, Rentham,' Mycroft said. 'Very observant of you, child. I did let someone into the room. And that *was* a liveried servant. But he came out immediately as there was no one inside.'

'No, he didn't,' Mary said. 'I never saw him leave, and I was watching all the time.'

'All the time? Even when you were apologising to the gentleman that you bumped into? It was you behind the column, was it not? I believe you spent a while speaking to him. You were not watching then. I believe that was when the person left.'

'But...' Mary fell silent. Mycroft Holmes was right; she had spent a good half-minute apologising and not looking. At the same time, she was sure no one left the room. She looked around pleadingly. However, with the exception of Archie and the small girls, there were no friendly faces to be seen.

'It appears, Rentham,' Mycroft Holmes said, 'that I may be inadvertently responsible for a part of this. No doubt the valet used his time to open the window to allow an accomplice to enter and prepare the safe.'

'But you were not to know,' Rentham said.

But he did know, Mary wanted to say. Now she thought about it, she was sure that he delayed Rentham from entering the room with his talk about paintings. Mary scowled inwardly. And why would the valet need to open the window? A swift kick from the outside would break the glass, and anyone could then sneak in. Mycroft Holmes was lying. Of that she was sure. Yet, why did a man of his stature—and no doubt exalted position, judging by how comfortable he appeared in the company of these important men—have need to lie?

His smile made her nervous. If the mood in the room was unfriendly, his smile caused the hairs on her arms to prickle. It was as if he knew her thoughts. She watched as he removed a tortoiseshell snuffbox from a pocket. He placed a few grains on the back of his hand, and as he raised it to his nose, his gaze never left her.

Mary's own gaze flitted across to a small table and several glasses of champagne on the tray the fair-haired young man carried. Beside it was his satchel. If she asked why Mr Holmes hadn't noticed the young man leaving the room without those items, she wondered what he would say. But with Rentham looking at her in the same way as Mr Holmes, her nervousness made her reluctant to mention it.

Archie broke into her thoughts. 'Mr Boots. Tell them about Mr Boots, Mary.'

'Miss Finch saw someone she recognised,' Lestrade explained. 'A Mr Boots.'

'Is he… known to you?' Mycroft Holmes asked the policeman.

'Indeed he is, sir.' Lestrade's ferret-like face brightened now that the attention of the room returned to him. 'From an incident of several months back. He was employed by a Mr James Grimwig; a blackmailer, we suspected, but alas, we could not prove it.' As he said this, the smile left Lestrade's face and he swung his head towards the shattered safe, a glimmer in his eyes.

'Blackmailer?' Mycroft Holmes said, loudly. 'But, of course. Rentham, do you not see? Do you not keep personal correspondence in that safe?'

'My personal correspondence is kept...' Rentham twitched nervously and he hesitated. 'Oh! Yes! Yes, of course.' He nodded several times. 'I... do keep... yes, I-I...'

'Well, that explains it,' Holmes said. 'There you have it, Lestrade. It is as you thought. The anarchists are branching out into blackmail. And who better to blackmail than Rentham?'

'But it weren't anar—' Mary begun saying.

'That was exactly my thought, Mr Holmes.' Lestrade interrupted her. 'Have no worries; we will hunt the culprits down.'

Mary stuttered in amazement.

'Mycroft,' Rentham said, 'perhaps your brother ought to be brought in—'

'Sherlock?' Mycroft laughed. 'No, no, no. This is something I am sure Scotland Yard can be trusted with. No, not Sherlock. Anyway, he is away on a case at this very moment and will not return for a good while yet. No, the good Inspectors Lestrade and Gregson will make a formidable pair in investigating this crime, I am sure.'

Lestrade beamed happily. 'I believe you had a run-in with both Mr Boots and this mysterious young man you keep on about, Miss Finch, in the woods back there,' he said. 'That is what she told me, sir,' he added for Mr Holmes's benefit. Mary frowned.

'Are you injured, child?' Mr Holmes asked. 'There is some blood on your collar and your wrist is bruised.'

Mary's hand shot up. She felt her neck, and when she looked, her fingers were smeared with a little red. She could feel the dull ache of a cut that happened when the fair-haired man yanked her locket off. The chain nicked her when it broke.

An odd memory returned—in the midst of the commotion, the fair-haired man threw the locket back to her. She was still clutching it in her other hand.

Mary looked at it, caught her breath and shivered.

'Are you all right, child?' Holmes asked. Mary hardly heard him. 'A chair for the young lady,' he said. She sat down heavily, her eyes staring blankly ahead.

'It must be the excitement,' Lestrade said. 'The events of the evening have caught up with her. I need not question her more as she has told me what occurred.'

Mary's mind spun in confusion. She screwed up her mouth, tasting something bitter. Archie was holding a glass to her lips. Eighty-year-old brandy did not agree with her and she coughed when she swallowed some.

She became aware that Mycroft Holmes was watching her intently. While everyone else was busy fussing, he wasn't. It was the same way he'd acted soon after the bombs went off. The feeling she had before, that he knew what she was thinking, returned. From feeling cold, she now felt hot. She tried to conceal her thoughts by looking elsewhere. Even so, she could not help her eyes wandering down to the locket she was clutching. She had to be sure of what she'd seen.

Again, a shiver ran up her spine.

'Is there something amiss, child?' Mycroft Holmes asked.

The chain that was hanging down through her fingers wasn't broken. She quickly gathered it up into the palm of her hand. When she glanced up, Mycroft Holmes's gaze was fixed on her clenched fist.

6

WHAT FORTUNE AND ELLA
OVERHEARD

'BLIMEY, you look like death warmed up,' Archie said.

Mary, Archie and the two girls were alone in the room; everyone else left to inspect the site of the explosion: the gardener's hut. A maid was sent to find Mrs Grady, and soon, they would leave for home.

Mary arose nervously and went to the French window. Mycroft Holmes and Inspector Lestrade were walking towards the carriages. They were deep in conversation. The policeman, it seemed, had asked all the questions he deemed necessary, and now that he was charged with a task—to solve a case of potential blackmail—the bulldog in him was smiling happily. It was more so with the knowledge that he would be the lead investigator. After all, he received the brief ahead of his rival, Gregson. As he predicted, Gregson returned to say he'd lost his quarry in the roads and trees at the back of the estate. Lestrade made a show of his displeasure.

Mary unclenched her fist and looked at her mother's locket. An aunt gave it to her as a reminder of her parents—both had died in an accident. The locket was divided in two; she had one half, and was told her brother, Daniel Finch, had the other. Almost five years older than her, they were separated soon after the accident. She was barely three at the time and had not seen him since. She knew little about his life, and only recently she discovered that he was suspected of murdering his foster parents, the Fullers in Gravesend, where he lived with them. A police warrant was issued for his arrest. Mary always dreamt of a reunion, to be reunited again as a family, but a murder charge was the last thing she expected.

'Want some more?' Archie asked. He was holding the glass of brandy, the stem threaded between his fore and middle finger, the bowl resting on his palm, the same way Fairchild Rentham had done.

Mary screwed up her mouth. 'I'd prefer a cup of tea,' she said.

Archie inhaled the aroma and sipped the ancient liquid with a satisfied sigh. 'What came over you just now?'

'He was lying, that Mycroft Holmes, about everything,' she said.

'I trust your instincts, Mary, but it's Sherlock

Holmes's brother we're talking about.'

'Don't I know it!' Indeed, the very thought that the great Detective's brother could be mixed up in this seemed ludicrous. Yet she was sure of what she'd seen. 'And look at this place,' she flicked her head at the room. 'It took a bit of preparation to set up the safe, and the other man was in here only for a few minutes… but that Mr Holmes was in here for a lot longer.'

Archie furrowed his brow, clearly seeing where Mary was going with her thoughts.

'And this ain't blackmail,' Mary continued. 'Did you hear how quick he was to get Lestrade to think his way? He was leading him. Personal stuff? Letters and papers? My aunt! And Lestrade puts two and two together and gets five. That Rentham was going to say something about another safe he had.'

Archie scratched his head. 'Yeah, but even so—'

Fortune tugged Mary's dress and said, 'They stole a torpedo, Miss Mary.'

Mary looked at her puzzled. The maid, though, wore a perfectly serious face.

'What you on about?' Mary asked, just as Archie blurted out laughing, spitting the brandy across the front of his shirt. Fortune glowered and gave him a harsh stare, and Ella sniffed crossly.

'They took it out of the safe and ran away with it,' Fortune said to him with a huff.

'That's exactly what he said,' Ella confirmed and both

girls nodded.

'Who said?' Archie, still giggling, managed to ask. 'Do either of you know what a torpedo is?'

'Don't need to,' Ella said, in a strop. 'They took one from the safe—'

'—and ran off with it, the soldier man said,' Fortune finished.

Archie turned away, convulsed with laughter.

'We were listening,' Fortune said, clearly vexed.

'They were arguing about the torpedo that got stole,' Ella said.

'That small man was swearing, like… *He* said all his hard work had been pinched.'

'He said the German anarchists took it.'

Fortune affirmed it with a sharp *told-you-so* nod to Archie.

Both girls were about to speak when Archie said, 'All right, you two, trust me, they didn't steal a torpedo.' He started to giggle once more, but when he saw the look on Mary's face, his hand quickly covered his mouth as he struggled to keep his straight.

'What *is* a torpedo, Miss Mary?' Fortune asked, unwilling to speak to Archie. Her eyes slewed across to him and her pout and furrowed brow returned as she glared at the boy.

Mary shook her head. She'd never heard the word before. But she knew Archie had, judging by his behaviour.

Archie managed to control his humour and his face become serious. He took their hands and said, 'It's a very big bomb that travels underwater and sinks ships. Bigger than you, even bigger than me. So, you see, it couldn't have been that what got nicked.' His smirk returned.

'Oh!' the girls said together. They looked at each other, then at the safe, and then gave Archie an acidic glare. 'But they *said*—'

'Did you hear the word *plans?*' Mary asked. She recalled the large flat case the fair-haired man was carrying. 'Think carefully. Did anyone say that word? Or the word blueprint or designs, maybe?'

The girls contorted their lips as they thought. Each took a deep breath. Suddenly, Fortune turned to Ella.

'The soldier man said it, didn't he, Miss Ella?'

Ella's mouth dropped open and both girls nodded enthusiastically.

'That's right. He said the plans are gone.'

'That's right,' Fortune echoed, 'and something about them anarchist people.'

'What did they say?' Mary asked.

The girls turned eagerly to her. 'That someone better stop them selling it,' Ella said.

'I told you he was lying!' Mary said. 'That's what this is all about. I bet he even planned it. That's why he doesn't want his brother to investigate because Mr Holmes would find out the truth in a hurry. And that's the other thing: Mr Holmes ain't away. I saw him looking out of his window when we came to collect you this afternoon, Archie. I waved at him and he waved back.'

But Mycroft Holmes was probably as well a respected a man as anyone could wish for, so how could she challenge him? She shook her head, unable to make sense of his lies.

Archie sighed heavily. 'If he stole secret plans, well, isn't that, you know, treason? I mean, you gets locked in the Tower for that, don't you?'

'Hanged as well,' Mary added, glumly.

'And he's Mr Holmes's brother. And when the coppers catch them, there'll be a big trial, at the Old Bailey probably. Here, Mary, we'll be called as witnesses. I mean, you saw Mr Boots and that other man. They're bound to call you.'

Mary's face went white, the anger that coloured it simply drained away.

'I can't,' she whispered, hoarsely. Sitting down, she stared dumbly ahead. She looked up at Archie, shaking her head. 'I can't.'

'What'd you mean, you can't?'

Mary swallowed drily. She opened her clenched fist. 'Look.' She showed Archie what was in her palm.

'It's your locket and chain. The one that aunt gave you.'

'No, you ain't seeing.'

Archie picked it up. It looked as always—just half a locket with a photograph pasted inside. He shrugged.

'The picture,' Mary said. 'Mum had a picture of me when I was three in one half and a picture of Danny in the other half. When the locket was divided, I got the half with Danny's picture to remind me I had a brother.'

Archie looked. The photograph was of a small smiling girl.

'But if you've got… this half…'

Mary nodded. 'And the chain ain't broken,' she said. 'It was ripped off my neck.' She rubbed the cut she'd received as if to confirm she hadn't imagined it. 'But look—this one ain't broken.'

'Well, how comes you got this one?'

'Don't you see? That was Danny.'

'Your brother? The young—?'

'Who else could it have been?'

Archie stared once more at the locket.

'May… be…' he said slowly, then fell silent.

'It could only have been him,' Mary said. 'Just before you came and fought with Boots, he shouted *"Run!"* I thought he was telling Boots to get away, but he was talking to me. He didn't want me to get hurt. It must have been him. Who else could have this locket, and why else swap them?'

She recalled how intently he scrutinised it with that confused look on his face; she knew why now.

'Don't you see, Archie? They'll hang him as a traitor if I testify. They'll hang my brother.'

7

MARY HAS A REQUEST OF
CONSTABLE O'CONNOR

IT WAS a fretful night where the ghosts from the past were raised. They gathered on the journey back to Holland Park, slowly creeping into Mary's mind to make a home there, clamping her tongue tightly so the long drive passed in sombre silence. Then, when everyone was asleep, they announced their terrible presence, inhabiting her dreams and waking her several times during the night.

In her dreams, her mother and father, people she hardly remembered who were faceless in the light, were clear and distinct. Daniel Finch watched her from some corner of her mind, a shapeless grey shadow, yet she knew it was he. Cold water swirled around, swallowing her. She fell through the icy liquid, reaching out a hand to grasp for someone, only to see Daniel waiting patiently under the gallows.

Her cat, Oscar, fed up with having his sleep disturbed, leapt off the bed. Mary woke and watched the cat pad quietly to the wardrobe for the peace they both sought. But her mind would not be still.

It *was* he, her brother, she'd seen at Rentham's, she was sure of that. Who else could have given her the locket? She was so near… so tantalisingly near…

In the morning, Mary's sullen silence was not lost on Mrs Grady. The old lady did not intrude; she was just waiting, Mary suspected, for her to speak. Several times, she tried to summon up the courage, but fearful of what her words meant, she kept quiet. Ella, sitting opposite her guardian, watched Mary nervously.

The bomb at Rentham's party made the front page of the *Times*. The article spoke of anarchists trying to assassinate a good many of society's notables. The police were after several individuals, it reported, and the newspaper's information came from a reputable source high up in the circles of government.

Mary read the article twice, and each time she was baffled. There was not a single word about the robbery. Mary understood that the paper could not mention anything about stolen secrets, nor blackmail, yet why mention anarchists when it wasn't them? Then, of course, Mr Rentham had to say something—everyone saw the results of the bomb, and that could not be denied. How could he explain treason and not mention his stolen plans? And how could she contradict Sherlock Holmes's brother?

She was so deep in thought that she was barely aware of the plate she'd removed from the breakfast table slipping through her fingers. Mary watched as it shattered on the floor by her feet. She felt Mrs Grady's reaction before she heard it.

'Sit down!' Mrs Grady barked so loudly that both Mary and Ella jumped. 'You have been walking around with a face that could sour milk since last night. Now, tell me what the problem is before I have to purchase a new set of china.'

'Please, Mrs Grady,' Mary said, 'I can't tell you.'

'Can't tell me?' asked Mrs Grady. 'Nonsense. Now sit.'

Mary sat down. Gingerly, she twined her fingers together and stared dumbly at the table. She knew Mrs Grady would not say a word until she spoke.

'Please, Mrs Grady, I just need some time off to sort out something,' she mumbled.

'I would be disappointed if you did not ask for my help if you needed it,' Mrs Grady said.

'Please, ma'am, it's just, I can't explain. There are a few things I need to do. I'll understand if you want my notice—but I have to see to this first.'

'Your notice?' Mrs Grady asked, incredulously. 'Why should it come to that? I told you once before, Mary, I need a bright, resourceful, clever girl to work for me, so why would I want to lose someone like you?'

Mary was silent, and Mrs Grady reached out and took her hand. She held it for a while, then sighed loudly.

'You are trembling, child. You told me a while ago of your desire to search for your brother, Daniel. Perhaps this is a good time to find him.'

Mary was startled, unsure why Mrs Grady should mention Daniel when she had not spoken of him for months—not since the Denbie affair. She certainly did not mention him during their journey home last night.

'You will need some money. Ten pounds to start with, more will be available if needed—do not be shy to ask. As we agreed once before, we can both help each other.' Mrs Grady opened a purse and slipped ten gold sovereigns into Mary's hand.

'But how did you know?' Mary asked.

'Fortune will cover your duties until you return.' Mrs Grady, picking up a knife and a piece of toast, started buttering one side. 'If you have a plan, it's best you carry it out; otherwise, take some time to formulate one. In either case, spare me the remains of my good china, if you please.'

When she left the breakfast room, Mary turned to say thank you. She noticed Ella quickly looking away, her guilty gaze dropping quietly to the plate in front of her.

As she rode the omnibus on that blisteringly hot day, the horses pulling it slick with sweat, Mary contemplated the first of two things she needed to do. She needed to find Constable O'Connor. His beat was in and around the West End. She and he had become friends since they first met under inauspicious circumstances earlier in the year, when he had arrested her. Then, with Archie's help, she would find Mr Boots. He and Daniel were connected somehow, and she hoped one would lead to the other.

She remembered something Sherlock Holmes said regarding the Grimwigs' Butler. At the time, she was recovering from her former employers' attempts to kill her. He said something about a house he owned in west London. She would go there to search for him at some point.

She found Constable O'Connor sheltering from the sun under the awning of the Marshall & Snelgrove department store on Oxford Street. He was peering through the window at the display of ladies' fashion. Mary looked over his shoulders.

'Nah! It'll never suit you,' she said. 'Those sleeves are cut far too short for your hairy arms.'

'Ho, ho, ho,' he said. 'Very droll.' The large, gruff policeman turned slowly, took off his helmet and wiped his forehead with a handkerchief. 'The music hall lost a rare talent when you decided to become a maid, didn't it, Finch?'

'That's a good one, *Sergeant* O'Connor. Did you think it up all by yourself?'

'Still the comedian, are we?' he said. Calling the Constable 'Sergeant' was an old joke and it always made him smile. This time, though, the joke was on Mary, as he proudly turned sideways to show her the neatly sewn white stripes on his sleeve. Sergeant O'Connor did not say a word. He merely looked past her. His wide and happy smirk said all that was needed.

'No one deserves it more,' Mary said, extremely happy for him.

'Do you want something, Finch?' he said, knowingly. 'You're lucky I don't arrest you for loitering.'

'Yes, *Sergeant*, thank you, *Sergeant*, it's kind of you, *Sergeant*,' Mary said. Puffing out her chest, she snapped a salute and he smiled.

They walked into Oxford Street and along towards Marble Arch.

'Look,' Mary said, 'I can't tell you why, I just needs you to trust me, is all…' The policeman pouted his lips and rolled his eyes. 'Three or so years ago in Gravesend, there was a double murder. A Mr and Mrs Fuller were the victims and their adopted son was marked as the killer: Daniel Fuller. I just need to know what happened. I could go to the library and trawl through all the papers, but that'd take a year and a half, and you coppers would have all the details at your fingertips anyways, and I'm in a hurry.'

O'Connor stopped and considered what she'd said for a minute. Mary knew it was an odd request, and she was grateful when he did not enquire more closely.

'Well, central records would hold the information, I suppose,' he told her. 'But you can't just waltz in and get it. Even a copper can't without proper authorisation. You in trouble, Finch?'

'I swear I ain't,' Mary said. 'But I can't—'

'—tell me about it,' he finished her sentence. 'Yes, I get it.' He stopped and looked up at the sky, clucked and nodded. 'I suppose Stella could.'

'Who's she?'

'Someone I know who works in records.'

'Does your Nancy know you've got a fancy woman?'

'Again with the jokes,' he said. 'Stella's her sister. Now, me and she ain't gonna get in trouble, are we, Finch?'

Mary was quiet.

'I thought as much,' he muttered.

'I ain't got no rights—' Mary said, pleadingly.

'All right, all right, leave it before I get the whole sob story. I can see tomorrow's headlines: *Police Sergeant found crying in Oxford Street.* I'll see what I can do.' He heard Mary's sigh of relief. 'Blimey! You look like you've lost a shilling and found a penny. Meet me Thursday. I should have something by then.'

She said her thank you and went to Baker Street to find Archie. Soon, she was standing by the door of the pie shop. Before she went in, she waited a minute under Sherlock Holmes's window—the sound of his violin drifted out into the air. She considered speaking to him, but felt loath to do so. How could she tell him that his brother lied? That Mycroft was mixed up in the theft of plans that, if they were given to the wrong people, amounted to treason? Anyway, she had her own problem brother to consider. She desperately needed to find Danny and persuade him to give back what was taken. What good that might do, she was unsure, since a charge of murder was following him.

One thing at a time, she told herself and entered the pie shop.

Archie looked at her suspiciously, clearly not expecting to see her so soon after the previous night, and stopped what he was doing. His nose was a fine shade of red tinged with blue, but it wasn't broken, much to his relief.

They sat at one of the tables.

'Remember when I was recovering from my dip in the Thames,' Mary said, 'after Black Bob and Davey Tupper tried to kill us?'

'Don't remind me.'

'Well, Dr Watson said something about Boots. He said that Mr Holmes did an investigation, and wasn't it odd that a Butler owned a house in Barnes Green, out west?'

Archie nodded. 'I thought we'd agreed that Grimwig and Boots were in it together, blackmailing that Earl.'

Mary nodded back. 'They were—but what Mr Holmes was saying was that Boots is just a Butler. How many of them do you know who own houses? So, he probably bought the house with his share. If I'm gonna find Daniel, then that's the only place I can think to start. Sergeant O'Connor's giving me a hand—'

'Sergeant O'Connor?'

'Yes, he's been made up a rank now. And he's agreed to help me find out more about what happened in Gravesend.'

'The murders?'

'I need to know what really happened, Archie. I can't believe… well, you know what I'm saying.' Even though she did not know her brother, she could not bring herself to believe he murdered anyone. 'If I can get the notes on the investigations, there may be more clues there about Danny's friends, or something that'll give me other places to look if he's not in Barnes.'

'You don't want to speak to Mr Holmes first?' Archie asked. 'I mean, some of this concerns him, don't it?'

'And tell him what? Maybe when I know some more. Well, you up for it? Going to Barnes, I mean.'

'What's that thing Mr Holmes says? *The game's afoot?* Though what a foot has got to do with things, I don't know.' He giggled and Mary groaned.

'Dear me! You and O'Connor ought to become a double act at the Shoreditch Empire,' she said. 'You'd go down a riot.'

8

A PAIR OF BLACK EAGLES

THEY TOOK the train from Waterloo and alighted in Barnes beside the common, and walked across the open fields towards the river and the green. Mary hoped that the green would be a small affair with only a few houses. Since she did not know which one belonged to Boots, so the fewer, the better. Somehow, they would have to find it without alerting the Butler. Then she would speak to Daniel Finch, whom she hoped would be there.

What she would say, she did not know. Much depended on whether she guessed right, and if Boots was there as well. As long as she stayed outside and didn't go in, she felt she would be safe. Either way, Archie would be with her.

She looked at the locket. The moment he saw hers, Daniel must have known who she was—that together with the Butler shouting her name. She concluded, it was why he'd deliberately exchanged lockets, to let her know who he was. But why had he not tried to find her in all the time since they were apart? She had been so close to him, her fingers tingled with the knowledge.

But her worry returned. Not many months ago, Lorna Denbie, a clairvoyant, predicted Daniel was in danger. She'd not believed her. How could she? The Denbies were guilty of contriving a dreadful plan that involved murder, and their lies almost worked. Yet, before she vanished, Lorna insisted she'd spoken the truth.

Your brother is in great danger. Trouble surrounds him like a mist. I do not understand it—your brother is both a lie and a truth at the same time. He has embarked on a dangerous journey.

Even now, Mary did not know if she believed her—Lorna Denbie was a clever girl, an excellent con artist.

They crossed the common and were on the road leading towards the green. A row of houses was in front of them. The road curved towards other houses further along, edging both its sides. Just ahead lay their destination.

Mary's head was down as she considered Lorna Denbie's prediction, so much so, she didn't see Archie's urgent gestures. Only when he grasped her arm did she notice the concerned expression on his face. He flicked his head along the road.

Crouched behind a house could be seen several policemen. Across the road, others were hiding. Some carried rifles and were moving carefully and furtively. Others were hurriedly escorting some elderly women and a few children around a corner. All this was done in silence.

'The coppers know where Boots lives,' she said and her heart began pounding.

'They must have figured the same as us,' Archie said.

There came a crack. A shot had been fired. A few policemen dashed across the street ahead of them.

'They'll kill him,' Mary said. She started to run to where the policemen were heading, only for a hand to grip her arm.

'Slow down,' a voice said. Mary turned to see the tall tow-headed Inspector Gregson. He had hold of her arm, and he wasn't about to let go. 'Slow down,' he repeated.

'You're going to kill him,' Mary said.

'Not in a month of Sundays. We want them alive so they can hang. Now, what are you doing here?'

Before she could speak, there came several sharp cracks. Gregson yanked her back and away from the middle of the street.

'Stay here,' he ordered. Taking out a revolver and keeping low, he started off towards the gunshots.

Further ahead, Inspector Lestrade was pointing, directing some of his constables towards the side of a small house fronting the green. The windows of the house were dark, all except one on the first floor. That one was open, and Mary could just make out an arm holding a pistol protruding from a corner. She heard a crack, and Lestrade and his constables scattered in several directions.

'Go on,' she heard Lestrade shout. Using a pistol, he waved at a large policeman hiding behind the tall hedge at the front of the house. He immediately sprang up and bolted forward. He charged through the garden gate and flung himself against the front door. There was a sickening thud and the door splintered off its hinges as he fell through. At that moment, Lestrade rushed forward. He and a group of screaming men ran up the path and piled into the house. There came several sharp cracks from within, followed by a heavy silence.

Mary's heart galloped. She scrambled up and was about to rush towards the house when Archie grabbed hold of her

'Let me go!' Mary screamed.

'Stop it!' he hissed. 'You can't go.' He ignored her clawing fingers trying to prise his grip loose. 'You can't let them know he's your brother.' He spun her around and, wrapping his arms around her waist, pulled her down to the ground. 'Stop it, will you?'

Mary was breathing hard and trembling. Archie's grip was firm and unyielding. He would not let go. After a while, as she became steady and calm, he relaxed his grip. She felt flushed, her face hot. She feared that Danny had been killed; the house was deathly quiet.

Their small spat went unnoticed, everyone's attention

was elsewhere. The police were leaving their refuge and mingling in the street. People were in their front gardens or doorways or peering through windows towards what Mary now knew was Boots's house. They were speaking, but in whispers.

Slowly, she and Archie edged forward, almost creeping towards the silent building. They were three houses away when a Constable said that was as far as they were allowed. Before long, several members of the public joined them. Soon, a small but angry and agitated crowd gathered.

'What's going on?' someone asked the policeman.

'Read about that incident at Fairchild Rentham's house?' he said.

'Where those anarchists tried to blow up Prince George?'

'One of them's in there.' He pointed with his chin towards the house.

'There was no assassination attempt. Prince George wasn't even there,' Mary said, but no one was listening.

'I hope they shoot them,' an elderly woman said.

'Or hang 'em,' her friend replied.

All around her, people were whispering the news: one of the bombers was apprehended. She wondered how this could have happened before she even had a chance to speak to Danny. This was like a dream, like one of last night's nightmares. She felt as if she was drowning, gasping for breath, and the world was spinning before her eyes.

Mary looked down at the ground, took some deep breaths and, grasping Archie firmly, leant into him to steady herself. She wanted to cry.

A host of voices exploded around her as Lestrade emerged from the house. Mary was bustled around and carried along by the crowd. Fists were punching the air, the shouts becoming savage screams.

'Hang him!'

'Murderer!'

'Let us have him.'

'We'll see to him.'

'Keep back! Keep back!' a policeman shouted.

In the entranceway was the older dark-haired man Mary saw with Daniel that night. His face was bloodied and bruised, his shirt stained with dabs of red. His wrists were handcuffed together, and burly policemen held his arms.

'Keep them back,' Lestrade shouted to his men.

A path was cleared through the crowd. A black police van, complete with bars, pulled up near the house. Lestrade led the prisoner through the angry crowd and the guards bundled him unceremoniously into the back. The door was slammed shut and locked.

Lestrade, standing beside the carriage, was smiling. Surrounding him were several men with notebooks. He showed them a gun, indicating that it belonged to the prisoner, and they scribbled down whatever it was he was saying.

Mary worried that the house still contained the body of her brother. To her utter relief, the Inspector said there was only one person in the house: the prisoner. A camera flash pan flared and caught the proud Inspector's triumphant face. The journalists' reports would no doubt make the evening editions.

It appeared Mycroft Holmes was right—Inspectors Lestrade and Gregson were making a formidable pair in tracking down their quarry. Even as she thought that, she saw him: Mycroft Holmes. For such a tall, wide man, he managed to go almost unnoticed. He was standing near an official-looking black hansom cab, some way from where the crowds were. There was an odd humorous expression on his face.

Another carriage, an enclosed landau with its hood up, pulled into the road just behind Mary. Emblazoned on the door was a coat of arms, a black eagle with outstretched wings holding a shield that sported another black eagle. The driver hesitated and called down to the occupant. The curtains of the windows were drawn open and a distinguished face peered out towards the distur-bance ahead.

The gentleman's glance fell on Mycroft Holmes. The portly man took off his hat and gave a nod of the head, and the gentleman removed his hat and returned the politeness. They knew each other, that was clear.

The next moment, the curtains of the landau snapped shut and the carriage turned around and left. As it did, the black police van pulled away. Mycroft Holmes ascended into his carriage and he too left, without stopping to congratulate the Inspectors on their success.

Mary watched him leave.

9

A TRAITOR

PERHAPS IT WAS the headiness of their success, so drunk were they with their victory, that made Gregson and Lestrade either ignore or forget Mary's presence. They left her alone, much to her relief. If they asked why she was there, she couldn't very well tell them the truth.

Before both Inspectors left, Mary kept a close watch on the comings and goings about the house. Various items were removed, mainly small things, and then the immediate area was cleared of people. A soldier went inside and emerged carrying a suitcase, which he carefully placed in a carriage.

When she heard a policeman mention explosives, she turned to speak to him.

'Here, mister,' she said, 'who was the bloke you arrested?'

'Anarchist,' he announced. 'Here, look.' He showed

her a leaflet. 'This was in the house. See? The Anarchist League of Great Britain. Right loons! Apparently, according to him, we are all lackeys of the rich and we're gonna get our comeuppance come the revolution.'

'Revolution?' Mary laughed along with the Constable. 'Well, you lot pinching him was quick work. So much for his revolution!'

He nodded. 'We had a tipoff. There were meant to be three of them inside, but we only got the one. The other two legged it before we arrived. But don't you worry your pretty head, miss, we'll get them.'

'I don't doubt it,' Mary agreed, 'with Scotland Yard on the job.'

'Oh, it's not just us, but the bleedin' Home Office as well. Now there's something, when they get to talk to the prisoner before we do.'

'Blimey, he must be really important if they're involved. They'll probably put him on the rack, won't they?'

'That's for sure. Some Major from the Home Office briefed us this morning. If he hadn't delayed us, we'd have got them all. But I didn't like the look of him one bit—he's a ginger one, all right. I reckon if he has his way, that bloke will talk. He'd have hanged him as well if he'd shot any of us. Who knows, he might hang him anyway.'

'The Home Office taking over the investigation, ain't that unusual?' Mary asked.

'Taking over? Don't you believe that for one minute. This one is Scotland Yard's, not some bleedin' Home Office snoop wanting all the glory.'

Before long, the house was sealed and a guard placed by the door. By then, it was obvious to Mary that no large parcels, in particular, the leather portfolio she saw Daniel carrying, had been found. The plans were not there.

Something, however, still troubled her.

As she and Archie made their way back to Barnes station, Mary said little. She waited quietly on the platform and, when the train came, sat staring out of the window.

Her silence wasn't lost on Archie.

'What's nagging you?' he asked.

'Anarchists,' she said and huffed, 'that's what. The morning papers said anarchists tried to assassinate Prince George. Even the coppers back there were talking about anarchists. I mean, I know Lestrade thinks it was anarchists last night, but that bomb made no sense.'

'Mycroft Holmes seems to think it's them.'

Mary shook her head. 'You don't blow up a hut when there's a better target.' She continued to stare out of the window, but her eyes saw little. 'And there's the safe. Archie, what if Lestrade hasn't been told what was taken from the safe? I mean, never told about the plans.'

'What? He's the law. Of course, he's been told.'

'No, I mean, what if Mr Holmes and those others don't want him to know?'

Even as she said it, she recognised that it was an odd idea. But her mind was jumping from one thought to the next. She could not help but remember how strangely Mycroft Holmes acted: denying what she knew to be true, even leading Lestrade into believing the robbery was about blackmail.

'But why not tell them?' Archie asked. 'Doesn't make sense. Come on, Mary, this is about treason. How would the coppers not know?'

Mary gave him a weak smile and shook her head again.

'I don't know,' she said and fell quiet again.

No, she said to herself. *Some plans for a weapon have been stolen.* Fortune and Ella overheard correctly, of that she was sure. The plans would be sold and no doubt they were worth a King's ransom. Who would purchase them? A competitor? More likely another government. If that was so, she took a deep breath, it meant Daniel Finch *was* a traitor.

Even so, why did Mycroft Holmes not tell Lestrade what was missing? Surely that was far too important to keep from the police. But what had the Constable just said? The Home Office was investigating and some government snoop was leading the investigation. If Mr Holmes was so confident of Lestrade and Gregson, even above the ability of his brother, why did he feel it necessary to bring in this Major? That would have been his doing.

She turned back to Archie.

'He was there, did you see him?' Mary said.

'Who?'

'Mycroft Holmes. That don't make sense either,' she said.

'You've got a real bee in your bonnet about him, haven't you?' Archie grinned.

'Happened on the sixth chime!' Mary huffed. 'I didn't imagine it, Archie. I saw him with Daniel—'

'And you saw Daniel before, at that explosion in Greek Street—'

'Yes, but last night, I saw them together, and Mr Holmes lied about it. He knew what happened, I'd stake my life on it. He knew I'd seen them together. And did you see the other man he was with just now?'

Archie had not, so Mary explained about the landau. She thought the occupant were taken by surprise with what happened at Boots's house. The two men knew each other, why else would they bow so politely?

'Let me get this right,' Archie said, shaking his head slowly in disbelief. 'You think he, or they, was meeting Danny and Boots to get the plans from them? Sherlock Holmes's brother—a traitor? You said as much in Rentham's place last night, but I thought you were joking. Traitor? That takes some believing, Mary.'

Mary turned away. It both made and didn't make sense to her. The only thing she knew was how little she knew.

She remembered Dr Watson saying how Sherlock Holmes always spoke about data, the more you had, the better understanding you would have. If she was to find Danny, information was what she needed.

'I've been thinking, Archie. I need to go to Gravesend.'

'There's the one o'clock from Charing Cross, but we'll have to leg it across Waterloo Bridge and down the Strand if we're to catch it.' Archie winked at her. 'I thought you might want to do something like that, so I checked the timetable back at the station. What do you expect to find there?'

Mary gave a deep sigh and sat back in her chair.

'I don't know, really. But something's wrong and I can't sit and do nothing. It's just a hunch. Now that the coppers have raided Mr Boots's house, he and Danny are gonna have to find somewhere else to hide—'

'Which could be anywhere—'

'It could be. But I read somewhere that fugitives hide in places that they're familiar with. They're like wounded animals, finding a lair to feel safe in. Gravesend is where Danny grew up. And I need to find out what happened down there with him and the Fullers. It's a place to start, Archie, that's all I can say.'

Even as she spoke the words, she felt as if she was clutching at straws.

10

GRAVESEND

THE SUN WAS BEATING DOWN and the afternoon heat stoked up as Mary and Archie walked from Gravesend railway station towards the riverbank. There they stopped to sit on a wall and have a bite to eat. Afterwards, Archie went along to ask the people in the shops if they knew where the Fullers, Danny's foster parents, the ones he was suspected of murdering, were buried.

Mary gazed over the oily grey-brown Thames, deep in thought. A thin breeze blew in from across the water. Several fishing smacks drifted along, their sails hardly fluttering. A steamer was making its way up the river; the dark smoke billowing from its funnel rose lazily into the air and hung in a long almost static line of smudged blackness behind it. Two small warships were anchored towards the middle of the wide channel. One flew the

White Ensign of the Royal Navy, and the other a black and white flag she could not make out.

She finished her bottle of ginger ale and was just about to launch it into the river when Archie came back.

'They're buried in a churchyard outside of Gravesend,' he said of the Fullers. He sat down and took the bottle from her.

'Peaceful here, ain't it?' she said

'Too bleedin' so. Nothing to do except watch those gunboats over there and throw bottles into the river.' With that, he threw the bottle high into the air and they watched as it splashed into the oily water. It sank, and then bobbed up to the surface as the tide carried it along. 'The British one's HMS *Strike*. The other's one of the Kaiser's, SMS *Prinz Wilhelm* on a goodwill visit. It's here 'til Saturday.' Archie looked around and about him with some disdain. 'This place needs all the goodwill it can get. Must be murder in winter.'

Mary slipped off the wall and they walked towards the church of St Peter and St Paul. The stone rubble building decorated with a freestone dressing, several arched windows and a square tower with an embattled parapet lay a short distance away, almost hidden by tall trees. They wandered lazily amongst the gravestones. Most were decidedly old, dating back over a hundred years, and were moss-covered and worn. In places, time caused some to collapse or lean crookedly. The more recent stones were easy to see. Generally, they were bright and untouched by nature, the carving clean and precise.

Before long, Mary found the one she was searching for. A stone angel with folded wings, hands clasped together in prayer, gazed silently upwards to heaven. Below was a richly decorated plaque:

In Memory of Joshua and Cissie Fuller, died 3rd February 1890

In grateful remembrance of those who gave their universal goodwill towards their Comrades, this Stone is placed here at their expense as a small testimony to their regard and concern.

Mary knelt beside the stone and traced a finger along the words. So these were Danny's adopted parents. She wished she and her brother had been kept together after the accident that orphaned them, but fate had other plans. She went to the Chidewells in Southwark—and she'd been happy there until she had to leave—and Danny to the Fullers in Gravesend. She hoped he was happy with them, but that obviously wasn't the case.

'What happened, Danny?' she whispered. 'Why'd you kill them? They weren't that bad, were they?'

'I have not seen you before.'

A stout elderly man dressed in a cassock stood before her. His eyes were bright, and a pair of gold-rimmed glasses was perched rather precariously on the end of his nose. He was sweating profusely and his forehead glistened with perspiration.

'Hello, Vicar,' Mary said.

'Were you acquainted?' he asked.

'Well, after a fashion,' she answered. 'You see, they adopted my brother...' and she explained the circumstances.

At the end of her account, the Reverend looked around, a somewhat vague and absentminded expression on his face.

'Now, what was I doing?' he said, ignoring both Mary and Archie. 'Tilly, what was I doing?' he shouted.

A young woman appeared through the side door of the church. Her hair was pulled back severely and tied tightly in a bun; she was wiping her hands on her apron.

'Who knows?' she said and shook her head. 'Wanting your tea, maybe?'

'Tea!' He brightened. 'Is it that time already?'

'It's been that time for the last twenty minutes, Reverend. Come on in and I'll make a fresh pot. What did the doctor say?'

He waved his hand as if to shoo away the question.

'Tea for my guests as well, Tilly,' he said. Before Mary could say anything, he grasped her elbow and was steering her towards the door. 'Yes, yes, I remember Daniel well,' he said. 'A good boy. A kind boy. A clever boy. Killed them, did you know? But I don't know. Never found them, did you know?'

They entered a largish room somewhere at the back of the church. It was untidy with books and papers, an overflowing desk, several armchairs and a clear area where Tilly was boiling a kettle on a spirit stove.

'What you on about now?' she asked.

'The Fullers,' he said. 'They're dead, but they're not. Any biscuits, Tilly?'

'What did the doctor say, Reverend Eustace?' she asked, sternly.

Again he waved his hand to shoo away the question.

'Biscuits for my guests, you wicked child. This really will not do.'

Tilly sighed, shook her head again and took the lid off an ornately decorated tin.

'Old. Pre-dates the Doomsday book,' the Reverend said.

'What does?' Archie asked.

'The church, of course. That's why you're here, isn't it?'

'No, we came to see the Fullers' grave,' Mary said, a little confused.

'Ah! Why did you not say? A good boy, Daniel. A kind boy, a clever boy.' He nodded. 'Wasn't he, Tilly?'

'If you say so, Reverend.' Tilly, standing with her back to them, hunched her shoulders, glanced over, sighed once more, and then turned back to attend to the singing kettle.

'Of course, it's been built on since. The north gallery was extended in 1818, and the sanctuary and nave walls were tiled and new windows added in 1860.'

The Reverend nodded sagely. 'Yes, yes! I remember it well.'

'No, you don't, Reverend,' Tilly said as she poured hot water into the teapot. 'You weren't here then.'

He looked somewhat perplexed.

'No, you was abroad—'

'Abroad! Ah! The ships. You saw them? Anchored in the channel?' he said excitedly. 'One's German, did you see? I have relatives in Hamburg. That's in Germany, did you know?'

Mary smiled politely and glanced to Archie.

'Yes, yes. Lutherans.' He shook his head sadly. 'Lutherans. They trimmed the trees and tended the graves, did you know that?'

'The Lutherans did?' Mary was puzzled.

'Heavens, no! They never trimmed any trees that I can recall. Unless… in Hamburg—'

'The Fullers,' Tilly, suppressing a laugh, said to Mary. 'He means the Fullers.'

'What about them?' the Reverend asked. 'Ah! Wait, wait, I have a picture of them.' He was immediately up and searching through the pile of papers on the desk. 'I'm sure… I have… a photograph…'

Mary fidgeted uncomfortably as Tilly brought a tray over.

'He don't have one,' she whispered.

'Ah! Here it is,' he said. 'I knew I had it. This will interest you, young man. The tower is late medieval. Oh!

And the nave as well—' He was holding a small folding leaflet.

Tilly winked. 'Just nod,' she said and began to pour the tea. 'And the sundial, Reverend?'

'Mr James Giles, or was it Gilbert? Gideon? built it— ooh, eighteenth century, I expect. They're not dead. Never found them, did you know?' And he tapped his nose at Mary.

'Never found who?' Archie asked.

'Now, where's that leaflet, Tilly? Come, come. The one from… from… you know… you know…' and with that, he sauntered out of the room and into the main body of the church, holding the leaflet.

'That's the second brew,' Tilly moaned. 'Come on, have some and let's not have it go to waste. Sugar? Milk?'

'Is he all right, Tilly?' Mary asked.

'Polly,' she said. Mary was about to say '*What?*' when, 'Polly,' she repeated. 'Not Tilly. Tilly was a maid he had in Ceylon when he was a boy. He thinks I'm her, though apparently, she was as brown as a nut, so I don't know where the resemblance is. Then he'll remember and I'm Polly again. The man's daft as a brush, sometimes. He caught malaria in India ten years ago and it went to his brain. He came back and he's never been the same since.'

'Shouldn't he be in a hospital or something?' Archie asked.

'He is of sorts. He's been looked after in the vicarage by the present Vicar. He just wanders around and… well, you can see, can't you?'

'What's he going on about them not being found?'

Polly sat back in a chair and sipped her tea.

'Well, that's true enough. The bodies of the Fullers was never recovered. That's just a memorial stone out there with no one under it. They reckon that kid of theirs weighed them down with rocks and dropped them into the river.' Mary's eyes sank to the floor. 'And then he ran away. Nice boy. The Reverend's right about that. Daniel was his name. Helped out a bit after school and weekends. You never can tell with people, can you?'

Mary shook her head. 'Did you know him?'

'No,' Polly said. 'Not really. Saw him a few times, is all. Dead clever, I was told. Shame really. Everyone reckons he had the brains to do well.'

'What did the vicar mean, they're dead but they're not? Who's dead but not?'

Polly clucked and rolled her eyes.

'He—the Reverend—reckons he saw Mr and Mrs Fuller in Wells when he was there for a conference last year and had a chat with them. I mean, they had only been dead a couple of years, so why shouldn't he be having a chat with them?' She rolled her eyes again. 'Reverend Eustace was in Wells, but not at a conference. He wasn't as bad then as he is now, but that was about when I became Tilly and the Bishop decided to lay him off, or whatever it is you do to Vicars when you fire them. He's better in the mornings if you want to speak to him proper like, but after lunch, he's dancing with the fairies. So, how comes you know the Fullers?'

'Oh, it's a long story,' Mary said, evasively. 'Friends of the family, really.' She trailed off into silence.

'Then you'll know Bessie Grainger, Mr Fuller's sister, in Ridge Farm?'

'Bessie! Yes. I ain't seen her in ages, not since I was three or four.' Mary told the lie confidently. 'Can't remember her really. Never been to the farm, though.'

'Just follow the Milton Road a couple of miles towards Denton,' Polly said. 'You'll see the sign. It's a shame what happened to the Fullers, though. They never did catch him that did it.'

BESSIE GRAINGER

RIDGE FARM WAS a series of low-slung buildings surrounding an enclosed area. A rough path connected it to the Milton Road, a screen of trees guarding the Thames side against the worst of the weather blowing in from across the water. At the back of the farm, the land was flat and drifted away to a scree of stones that ran along the line of an embankment across the horizon. Beyond that, the sky was endless.

Mary saw her watching as they made their way along the Milton Road. A stocky woman in her fifties, a wide infectious smile on her lips, was standing in the doorway of the small cottage. Her plump face was dry, weather-beaten and ruddy as if she had been in the sun for several hours. The woman did not move, even as Mary and Archie crossed a rickety wooden bridge over a small watercourse that ran beside the road. Not even as they stepped on to the path that led to her house.

But after Mary introduced herself, the smile faded and her face took on a puzzled look. However, she invited them in for tea, saying her name was Bessie.

The room they were in was sparse and untidy. Dust lay on all the surfaces and the windows needed cleaning. The carpet needed a good brushing and the chairs were dingy. A glimpse through a door showed the unwashed dishes on the kitchen table. And amongst all of this was Bessie, with her dirty clothes and apron, and the faint odour suggesting she needed a bath. Mary couldn't help but feel sorry for her.

As Bessie made tea, she hustled and bustled between the kitchen and where Mary and Archie sat. Her smile reappeared.

'Well, bless me!' Bessie said. 'You're the sister. Dear me, you're she. My goodness, there was a time when he wouldn't stop gabbing about you—Mary, isn't it?'

Mary beamed brightly, realising Daniel remembered her, after all.

'But you died,' Bessie said.

It was time for Mary's smile to vanish.

'Years ago—my brother, Joshua brought us news that you'd died.'

'But missus, I ain't dead,' Mary said, somewhat confused.

'Well, I can see that, can't I! And look—you've even got the other half of his locket, so it must be you.'

Mary clutched the locket, knowing that it was Daniel's half she held.

'But why did Joshua say that?' Bessie said to herself. She laid the cups on the table, and as she stirred the teapot, her eyes squinted. She shied back. Her face held a doubtful look, and suddenly, she became angry.

'You're not tricking me, are you, young lady? If it's money you're after, Joshua didn't leave any. The house was sold to pay off his debts, so there's nothing to claim.'

'Mrs Grainger, I ain't no money-grubber,' Mary said. 'I just want to find out about Danny and what happened.'

'Sam warned me about people like you.' Bessie rose to her full height. 'He said you would come…'

'No, no, Mrs Grainger. I swear I ain't after any money.' Mary crossed her heart.

Bessie Grainger hesitated and sat uncomfortably on the edge of her chair as Mary, speaking thirteen to the dozen, explained how she and Daniel were separated and what happened to her since that time. As she spoke, the smile that seemed to fit so comfortably on Bessie's face returned once more. By then, the tea was lukewarm, but no one seemed to mind.

For a while, Bessie sat deep in thought. She then spent a few minutes looking at Mary as if examining her before deciding she had been told the truth. Even so, when she eventually spoke, she still seemed troubled.

'But Joshua said you were dead,' she repeated in confusion. 'Passed away in Liverpool. Danny was so upset… he used to always be speaking about you, and afterwards… well, he just stopped. He was so sad. Then he sort of went into his self.'

'I was in Liverpool,' Mary said, 'I was taken there by Mrs Chidewell once. But it weren't me that died, missus. It was a friend, from Cholera.'

Suddenly, Bessie started speaking about Daniel. She talked non-stop for almost ten minutes. As she talked, Mary had the distinct impression that Bessie had few friends and was glad of the company.

'He was such a good kid,' Bessie ended. 'So helpful and smart. Joshua used to call him Quicksilver because of how quick he was on the uptake.' She shook her head as if forgetting she had company. 'You were such a hard taskmaster, Joshua. It weren't right… Here, the tea's cold. Let me make a fresh brew.' Bessie was just about to rise when her face brightened. 'Your dad!' she said, her eyes shining. 'Oh, Danny took after him—just as bright, just as curious, and looked just like him, too, he did.'

'You knew my dad?' Mary could barely remember him.

'Aye, and your mum—a handsome couple if ever there was one.' Something, though, was troubling Bessie. It was written plainly on her face. Noticing, Mary looked over to Archie, who shrugged.

'What is it, missus?' she asked.

Bessie swallowed nervously. 'I can't say, luv… I mean, no one knows, and I can't tell you anyways.'

'Tell me what, missus?' Mary asked.

Bessie sat back quietly, a faraway look once more on her face, and did not say a word, even when Mary asked her again what she meant. Slowly, Bessie's eyes closed and she seemed asleep. But Mary knew she was deep in thought.

It appeared as if she would say no more. Mary, thinking they should leave, was quietly rising from her seat when suddenly Bessie's eyes popped open.

'Wait, wait, wait,' she said hurriedly. She grasped Mary's hand, pulling her down again as if wanting her to stay. Bessie arose quickly and crouched beside a small cabinet. She pulled at a drawer that opened partially, twisted at an angle and became stuck. Struggling with it, Bessie cursed under her breath and pulled harder. It sprang loose and she tumbled backwards, the contents spilling across her lap. Archie rose to help, but she waved him back, fencing his arms away in a disgruntled manner.

When she stood, she was clutching a small bundle tied with a ribbon.

'Look, look, these are them,' she said and waved the bundle as she sat down. 'I always meant to put them in an album.'

Bessie was struggling to untie the ribbon around a wad of photographs, letters and postcards, and only succeeded in making the knot tighter. In frustration, she eventually slipped the ribbon aside and slid the contents out. She patted the seat beside her for Mary to sit.

'Your dad,' she said, looking up at Mary kindly.

Mary fell silent. She took a deep breath and shivered as she looked at the photograph the woman was holding. It was unmistakably him, her father, just as he looked in the only two photographs she had of her family. The man beside him, Bessie said, was her brother, Joshua Fuller. They were posing in what seemed to be a shipyard.

Bessie sat back and handed Mary the loose pile, closing her eyes again. Her lips moved silently as if she was praying. Mary looked at the photographs in silence, a shiver running up her spine again. There were only a few, but several were of her father, some with a woman Mary knew to be her mother. She recognised Bessie standing with her husband—or so she assumed him to be—as well as Bessie's brother and wife, Danny's foster parents. Out of respect, she did not read the letters amongst the pile, but carefully placed them aside.

'Archie,' she said, 'it's Mum and Dad...'

Archie came and sat beside her. He placed his arm around her shoulder. Mixed up amongst the photographs were several postcards and Christmas cards going back for many years. Mrs Grainger kept and stored them carefully, things from her past; things that probably made her happy. She carried the air of a lonely woman, and Mary wondered if, every now and then, Bessie took them out to remember those times long since gone.

As Mary scanned the Christmas cards and postcards, she became puzzled. She turned one of the cards over. It was a picture of a magnificent, a perfectly symmetrical cathedral surrounded by trees. She returned to the inscription.

'Bessie, it's in the papers,' a voice boomed from the kitchen, followed by a loud, triumphant barking roar and the slamming of a door. 'Anarchists tried to kill Fairchild Rentham, it says. And they've caught one. That gunboat—'

A small pug of a man, wrinkled and unshaven with a broad, flat nose, bounded into the room, waving a newspaper. A face that seemed unused to smiling immediately set itself into an angry scowl and the croak that passed as a laugh died on his lips. His eyes took in the room, glancing first at Mary, and then at Archie, his wife, and eventually the drawer and its contents on the floor. He was leaning heavily on a cane that he slowly lifted.

'S-S-Sam…' Bessie Grainger awoke with a startled snort. She gasped for breath and a furious trembling washed over her.

'Who the hell are these people?' Mr Grainger said. 'You heard me, woman—who the hell are they?'

12

MORE QUESTIONS THAN ANSWERS

BESSIE STAGGERED towards him with a frightened, guilty look on her face.

'Sam, look, it's—'

'Bringing strangers into the house?' Samuel Grainger barked. 'Is that it? Strangers? Is that what it's come to?' He pointed the cane towards Mary and Archie as a threat.

'No, no, you don't understand, Sam, it's—'

'Can't I leave you alone for a minute?' he shouted. 'What did I tell you, woman?'

'But, Sam—'

The cane rose higher.

'Stop bullying her.' Archie sprang forward. He grabbed the cane. 'I said, let her be,' he shouted.

Grainger swung around. The boy was at least half a head taller than him and doubt came into Grainger's eyes. Even so, he tugged at the weapon and spat out several curses. Unable to free the cane from the boy's grip, he aimed a punch at his head. Archie swayed easily out of the way and tugged hard on the stick. His lame leg collapsing, Grainger tumbled to the floor. When he looked up, Archie was standing over him holding the cane.

'Leave her be,' Archie shouted. 'She ain't done nothing wrong.'

'That's assault,' Grainger cried in panic. He raised his hand to shield his head as if expecting the cane to descend on him. 'I'll get the law on you, boy. You'll go to jail. Hard labour for you—'

'Sam, it's Mary,' Bessie Grainger shouted through her tears.

'They don't take kindly to young 'uns assaulting the elderly,' he carried on. 'They'll lock you up. I know your face, boy. I know the judge—'

'Sam, Sam, it's Mary,' Bessie cried again. 'Danny's sister. Mary Finch.'

Samuel Grainger froze and fell dumb, his mouth open in the middle of delivering another curse. Slowly his eyes widened and slipped across to the girl hugging his crying wife. He silently mouthed Mary Finch's name.

When he found his voice, it was panicked. 'What you been saying, woman?'

'Nothing, Sam, I ain't said nothing.'

'Don't you lie to me.'

'I ain't, Sam. All I did was show her some pictures of her dad.'

Grainger looked towards the pile of photographs and cards on the low table.

'Get me up, boy, get me up now.' He held his arm up towards Archie. Archie hesitated. 'Help me up, I say.'

The fight had gone out of Sam Grainger.

'Help him, Archie,' Mary said.

Archie glared at him. 'I don't take kindly to a woman getting threatened,' he warned Grainger before extending his arm.

Once standing, Grainger spent several moments watching Mary carefully. When Archie held the cane out for him to take, he snatched it quickly and gave a low snort. By then, his wife had stopped crying and was sitting peacefully with her head bowed. He hobbled over to the low table and cast his eyes across the papers and stood straight.

'What else she told you?' he asked nastily.

'That I'm dead,' Mary replied.

His face twisted into an ugly scowl.

'Seems you ain't—if you're she.'

'It's her, Sam,' Bessie mumbled and went quiet when his eyes fell on her.

'Don't pay her any mind,' he said. 'She talks for the sake of talking. Didn't I tell you not to speak to anyone, Bessie?'

'But, Sam—'

'Who sent you?' he asked Mary.

'Sent me? What do you mean?'

'Who you working for?' Grainger licked his dry lips, his eyes fixed on her. Mary's brow furrowed in confusion. Suddenly, he too appeared confused. 'So, what do you want, then? Money?'

'I just want to find out what happened to Danny,' Mary said.

'What do you know?'

'Just that Danny is supposed to have killed some people, but I can't believe—'

'That he'd do something like that? The little you know of him!'

Mary gritted her teeth, an angry wave washing over her.

'That's right,' she shouted. 'I don't know anything about him, that's why I'm here, to find out.'

'There ain't much to tell,' Grainger said. 'Your brother turned nasty one day and killed his stepparents, and then dumped their bodies in the river so they could never be found and given a Christian burial. Now, get out of my house. I ain't having nothing to do with murderers, thieves and anarchists.'

'Me neither,' Mary said.

He scowled. 'Get out, I say.'

'You listen here, mister.' Archie stepped forward only for Mary pull him back.

'Let's go, Archie,' Mary said. 'We're done here.'

Archie fixed a deep stare on Grainger until Mary pulled his arm again. Then they both left. For a second, Mary waited on the front porch and took in a deep breath to calm her anger. Inside the house, she could hear an argument erupt.

'What did I tell you?' Sam Grainger was shouting. 'You don't tell anyone anything, isn't that what I said? The coppers are the last thing we need.'

'But she ain't a copper, Sam.'

'You don't know what she is, you stupid woman. Damn it! What do you think this is? A game? I should have known not to tell you anything.'

Bessie Grainger was crying again. Archie turned on his heels and pushed at the door, only for Mary to pull him away.

'We've got to go,' she said.

Archie hesitated. His fists were balled and his mouth was set firm.

'Archie, we've got to go,' Mary repeated, softly.

The boy reluctantly turned and they walked away, back towards Gravesend and the railway station. Mary could see he was seething.

'If the Fullers were anything like *him*, I wouldn't blame Danny for killing them,' he grumbled angrily. 'I bloomin' would. You should have let me thump him. I hate bullies. I'd have enjoyed that.'

Mary, though, was quiet. Other thoughts occupied her mind.

'No wonder he doesn't want the coppers—they'd give him the hiding he deserves before they arrest him,' Archie fumed. He continued, on and off, in that vein until they arrived at the station.

There was a half-hour wait for the next train and they sat quietly in the waiting room. Archie rested his elbows on his thighs and stared down at the floor between his feet. He was finally calm, but for the occasional grouch.

'Shouldn't we look some more, to make sure Danny's not here?' he asked.

'No, he ain't here,' Mary said. 'If he was, someone would know. You saw the place, it's too small to hide in. No, he's still in London somewhere.'

Unable to settle, Mary arose and wandered around the small waiting room. She read the posters and looked out of the window. Before long, she stepped outside and walked slowly up and down the street, deep in thought. She saw Sam Grainger entering the Post and Telegraph Office. He limped awkwardly with his cane, but went as fast as he could. He appeared worried. She hoped Bessie was all right.

She bought the morning and evening edition of the newspaper Grainger carried on his arrival home when she heard the whistle of the London train coming into the station. Hurrying back, Mary ran into three men on the pavement. They were wearing blue and white uniforms. Briefly, they got into each other's way, the men laughing loudly in the confusion as each tried to avoid bumping into her. One of them, a satchel around his shoulder, reached out and took her arm. Slipping a hand around her waist, he effortlessly twirled her out of the way as if they were dancing. Then he removed his cap and bowed deeply.

'*Sie tanzen hervorragend, Fräulein.*' He and the others laughed.

Mary staggered back. 'M-m-my train…' she stammered, blushing heavily and rushing into the station, ignoring Archie, who was also laughing.

13

A DEATH THAT ISN'T A DEATH

THEY FOUND an empty carriage and Mary collapsed into her seat. As the train pulled away, she watched the three men walking side by side towards the water.

'Archie, what was the name of that German ship in the channel?' she asked.

'Prinz Will—something or other. Wilhelm!'

'Those sailors just then, that was where they're from. The name was on their caps. The one who—you know, him.' She blushed again. 'On the satchel he was carrying, there was a crest. Did you see it?' Archie shook his head. 'It was a black eagle holding a shield on which was another black eagle. I've seen that crest before. Just this morning. The man Mycroft Holmes bowed to, the one in the carriage in Barnes, had it on the door of his landau.'

She fell silent. It was a curious thing, Mycroft Holmes acting so secretively, especially so soon after the theft of secret plans. And near the home of one of the thieves, as well. He obviously knew the distinguished gentleman who turned up there, the German gentleman.

And isn't Mr Holmes a good Englishman?

'What do you think he does, Archie? Sherlock Holmes's brother, I mean,' Mary asked.

'Something important, that's for sure, the way everyone was talking to him at Mr Rentham's, and him to them. Didn't you say he and Mr Rentham were discussing some government business? I reckon he's probably Minister for So-and-so or What-not.'

'No, not a Minister—I've never seen his name in the papers before.'

Mary spent a few minutes gazing out of the window as the countryside rushed past before fishing inside her pocket and taking out several pieces of paper.

'And that's not all,' she said.

Archie looked over. 'What's them?' he asked.

A somewhat embarrassed Mary showed him.

'Bloomin' thief!' Archie joked.

'Well, what are they going to do with them?' Mary had surreptitiously slipped two of Bessie Grainger's photographs into her pocket. One was of her father with two men, the other was of her father and mother.

'Well, that'll add to your collection,' Archie said. 'What's that, four in total?'

Mary nodded. Four photographs were now all she had of her parents. She was annoyed that she didn't taken more, but if she did, she feared it would have been noticed.

'I don't think anyone will miss them,' Archie said reassuringly, as if reading her mind. She felt relieved, then handed him another item she had taken. It was the postcard of the splendid cathedral. Archie looked at the image, shrugging his shoulders as if to say *'So?'*

Mary shook her head, her expression serious. 'I worry about you sometimes.' She pointed at the writing on the front: *Wells Cathedral.* 'Read the message.'

Archie turned it over.

Dear Bessie, all's well, we're settled in nicely, happy belated birthday, sorry we missed it, Joshua and Cissie.

Again, Archie shrugged.

'So, it's from the Fullers, when they went to Wells presumably.'

'Look at the post date, Archie.'

The boy's mouth dropped open. 'June, 1891.'

'What was the date on the Fullers' gravestone?'

'February… 1890,' Archie said quietly.

'When do dead people send postcards?' Mary asked. 'And Polly said the Vicar told her he saw them in Wells last year when he was at a conference there.'

'No, no, wait a second,' Archie said. 'They've got a grave and witnesses, and…' he shook his head. 'And there's no bodies in the grave, is there? It's a memorial stone only. And you're thinking that the witnesses to the so-called murder were the Graingers.' Archie read the inscription on the card again and shook his head slowly. 'All right, I'm lost. What's going on? I mean, if they ain't dead…?'

'Then they ain't dead, is what. That ain't all,' Mary said. 'What was it Mr Grainger said? He's having nothing to do with murderers, thieves and anarchists.' Archie nodded. 'Who told him Danny thieved anything or that he's an anarchist?'

'It's in the paper—the one he was reading.'

'No, it ain't.' Mary handed Archie the newspapers. 'I had a look. It's just as I read in the *Times* this morning. In neither edition is Danny's name mentioned. Anarchists at Rentham's party are, but there's nothing at all about theft.'

'Then how did he know?'

'I wish I knew. The Fullers aren't dead. The Graingers know that. They know a lot more as well—'

'And they ain't telling.'

'Mr Grainger ain't, that's for sure. Bessie would have. What secret was it she couldn't tell me, that no one knows?'

'Some insurance scam? Or confidence trick?' Archie suggested.

Mary looked doubtful.

'Don't make sense. I mean, the Fullers are meant to have died three years ago, plenty of time to settle any claims. If there's money involved, the Graingers didn't benefit. Danny neither. He's wanted for murder.'

'Except they're alive.'

Mary clenched her fists. 'I knew it, Archie. Danny's no killer!' she said happily. Then her face darkened and she whispered, 'But what is he? Something strange is going on. I'm more worried than before. I just wish I knew what's happening.'

'Whatever it is, it's as clear as mud!' Archie said and hunched his shoulders. 'What about telling Lestrade? Tell him about the Fullers, he'd be interested, wouldn't he?'

Mary sighed and sat back.

'I'm hardly in his good books, am I? Not since what I did to him in the spring.' Archie giggled and Mary gave him a stern glare. 'And he weren't best pleased with me at Rentham's place, either, was he?'

'Not when you told him how everything happened. No, not best pleased with you doing his job.'

The train clacked on and Mary sat gazing out of the window. Her thoughts returned to Danny. So that was why he never came looking for her—he thought she was dead. She chided herself—perhaps she should have searched for him instead. At least, before now.

The sky clouded over from the west, the direction they were heading, becoming overcast, dark and heavy. Soon, the first drops of water splattered the windows, and then the clouds burst and the rain sheeted down.

14

THE BAKER STREET
IRREGULARS

ONCE THEY ARRIVED BACK in London, Mary and Archie parted company, agreeing to meet back at the Dibbles' pie shop later on. Mary, in the meantime, had some errands to run.

By the time she returned to Baker Street, it was gone nine in the evening and she was soaked. Grandma Dibble found her some dry clothes, and after changing, Mary tucked into a warm, filling meal. Then she slept fitfully in her old room at the back of the shop. It was too late to go to Mrs Grady's in Holland Park, and she had an early start in the morning—or so she hoped.

The next day, as she went down into the shop for breakfast, she saw them just as she'd expected. Half a dozen or more boys, ill-dressed and not particularly clean, of various sizes and builds were leaning against or peering through the pie shop window. When she opened the door, they all came in at a rush, more than a few greedily eying the dishes left over from yesterday, sat behind the glass counter.

'We're looking for a Mr Finch,' the tallest of the boys said. 'I got a message to meet him here.'

'I left the message,' Mary said. 'And he's a she.'

'Oops! Pardon me, miss,' and he quickly removed his cap. 'The message didn't say you was a she.'

'And who are you?' Archie positioned himself between the counter and the boys.

'This is Wiggins, I should imagine,' Mary said, and the boy gave a neat bow at the mention of his name. 'And these are what Mr Holmes calls the Baker Street Irregulars, if I'm not mistaken.'

'That's us!' Wiggins said, proudly.

'Mr Holmes swears blind by them, Archie. He says they can come and go where others can't. No one really sees them, no one notices them. If you want something found, then these will find it for you—or find him for me.'

'A manhunt, is it?' Wiggins rubbed his hands together with relish.

'Two men,' Mary said. 'One called Daniel Fin—I mean, Danny Fuller—and the other, Boots. Cameron Boots used to be the Butler at the Grimwigs' place, up Regent's Park way.' Mary then gave the boys a description of the two men. 'All I know is that they're probably holed up somewhere in the centre of London, and they're probably alone.'

Wiggins scratched his head. 'That's a tall order, miss. It's a big area to cover.'

'Well, if you can't manage it—'

'Now, hold on a minute,' Wiggins said, quickly. 'I didn't say we can't, did I?'

'I know Bootsie,' one of the boys said and stepped forward. 'Me and my sister had a run-in with him some months back.' He was standing next to a dirty-faced girl, the smallest of the Irregulars who was almost hidden from view, dressed in breeches that came down to just below her knees.

'Yeah,' she said, 'we know Bootsie all right! He gave Freddie a thick ear and a walloping all because I asked him for a ha'penny. He'd no right to do that.'

'Here, miss,' Freddie's face brightened, 'weren't it his house that got raided in Barnes yesterday? That's what that copper was saying.' Suddenly his eyes bulged wider. 'Here, we after anarchists? That's more meaty than the usual stuff for Mr Holmes.'

'Is that why you want them?' Wiggins asked.

'It's my business why I want them,' Mary said, sharply.

'Yeah, but it's us doing the looking,' he said.

Mary sat back against the table and looked straight at Wiggins.

'I'll pay Mr Holmes's rates for three, maybe four

days looking, even if you don't find them. And that means no questions asked.'

'And where you gonna get the money?' Wiggins sneered, looking her up and down.

Mary took out her purse and slammed it down on the table. It made a resounding thump and rattle. Immediately, everyone's eyes fixed on her hand holding the purse.

'Well?' she said.

Wiggins nodded.

'All right, then. A shilling a day each,' he said, 'except for Kitty, she gets a tanner, and a sovereign for whoever finds them.'

'Oi! Why do I only get sixpence?' the small girl shouted and stepped forward. 'I do as much work as anyone else, and I've seen Bootsie and can recognise him, and I can speak to maids and you lot can't, and everyone knows maids tells more than butlers.'

'Because you're a girl, that's why. And you're new and I'm in charge, and I say who gets paid what.'

'That ain't fair, Wiggins.' The girl scowled and folded her arms.

'She gets a shilling,' Mary said. Wiggins glared at her. 'Don't give me that look either—it's my money and I'm paying. Now, do you want the commission or not?'

Wiggins smiled broadly. 'As you say, miss, you're paying. That's a day's wages in advance.'

Mary tipped out the required amount and gave each boy and Kitty a shilling.

'If you find them, report back to me or Archie,' she said.

'Don't suppose you can spare a slice of pie, mister?' Kitty said to Archie. Her eyes slewed over to a plate where a large pork pie rested, her face becoming sad and pathetic. 'All this looking'll be hungry work.'

Archie tightened his lips into a firm straight line.

'And a taste of ginger ale for the whistle, maybe?' Kitty added. 'Cor! Dry as a desert, me,' she whispered hoarsely to Freddie, her brother, loud enough so all could hear.

Mary managed to suppress a grin and nodded to Archie. Her friend gave Kitty an uncompromising look that said the pie was all she was going to get as he removed the dish from behind the counter. Immediately, he was surrounded. Almost as soon as he gave each a piece, it was consumed.

'Thanks, Missus,' Wiggins said. 'Do you want me to give him out there a slice as well?'

Mary was confused. Wiggins edged her over to the window and pointed along the street.

'Over there. See the gate to the basement flat? Can you see him?'

Mary squinted. She could just make out from the well of the flat, at pavement height and in the shadows, a face looking their way. The man wore a bowler hat. A wisp of cigarette smoke rose around him.

'I reckon he's a copper, judging by his size-twelve clodhoppers—shines them any more and he could use them as mirrors.' Wiggins laughed. 'Saw him when he came. He's been keeping an eye on the shop since we arrived. I reckon it ain't us he's eying.'

With that, Wiggins and his Irregulars left the shop. They stood for a few moments on the pavement as Wiggins said something to them. He pointed in various directions, and then they all rushed off.

For a full minute, Mary watched the basement well. She chewed her lip, wondering why someone should be observing her, before dragging her eyes away.

'Now all we have to do is wait.' She sighed, because waiting wasn't something she liked doing. Her fingers itched, her mind buzzed, her feet wanted to go some-where, and much to her frustration, she could do little for the moment.

'How do you know Danny ain't passed on the plans?' Archie asked.

'Probably not that easy to do now that the coppers have raided their hideout. Danny and Boots will need to be careful,' Mary said. She came back from the window and sat down. 'I was thinking the same last night. Lestrade thinks private papers have been stolen, and this is about blackmail. He'll know that the anarchists won't be doing the blackmailing, but will want to sell to those that will.'

'One of the embassies, you mean? Except he doesn't know it's plans.'

'Yes. If I were Lestrade, that's where I'd be keeping my eye—the Russian, German, Italian embassies. They're the ones who'd be interested in Rentham. I'd be following any official-looking people who leave them, to see if they meet up with anyone, and stopping anyone who vaguely resembles Danny and Boots from entering.'

'What about if he sells to one of Rentham's competitors?'

'It's possible…' Mary shook her head. Her brows furrowed and her eyes narrowed as she remembered the two men at Barnes Green and the black eagles. 'But I can't help thinking it's another country he'd want to sell to.'

It was treason they were discussing, of course. She was glad Danny was not a murderer, but the alternative seemed just as bad.

'And anyway, if they're watching me, then it means that they ain't caught up with Danny yet.'

'What makes you say that?'

Mary shook her head. 'Just a feeling I've got.'

She glanced back to the window and towards the basement flat, a worried look on her face.

'Well, God help Danny if they catch him,' Archie said.

THE BOWLER HAT AND THE
VANISHING STRIPES

THE DAY PASSED QUIETLY with no word from Wiggins. Mary fretted. There was little she could do but wait.

It soon became clear that she was being followed. Each time she left the shop, she could swear that someone was behind her. But when she turned to look, she could not see him. At first, she thought it was her imagination, but Wiggins's revelation about the man in the basement sat prominently in her mind. The thought of being spied on, and by the police, made her nervous.

Taking a basket, she left the pie shop and wandered to Oxford Street. She purchased some fruit and a few small items Grandma Dibble was short of, and then wandered back slowly. Every now and then, she stopped and gazed at the display in a shop window, sometimes slipping inside the shop for a closer inspection. However, she was not looking at the display, but at the reflection in the glass or, once inside the shop, past the display to see who was in the street.

The man following her was burly, wore a bowler hat and bright shiny boots, and tried not to be noticed. When she returned to the pie shop, he took up his sentry duties once more. When night came, another person replaced him. Come the morning, he was back again.

It was Thursday and Mary had an appointment with Sergeant O'Connor, and the last thing she needed was to be followed. At lunchtime, she left Baker Street, confident that her shadow was not far behind, and walked to Piccadilly. There, she went into the Swann & Edgar's department store. He followed her, as she thought he would. She chose a dress from a rack and went into the changing rooms. Once there, she left the dress on a chair and quietly exited by a side door and down the back stairs. Slipping her shadow was easily and deftly done, and she felt a surge of triumph.

She found Sergeant O'Connor once again under the awning of Marshall & Snelgrove in Oxford Street, this time sheltering from the drizzle that was falling on and off all day. His cape was around his shoulders and he looked grumpy. She was about to make a joke when he pulled her along and into a side alley.

'I stuck my neck out a long way for you, Finch,' he growled, 'and I distinctly felt a cold, cold breeze on the back of it. Now, what have you got me mixed up in?'

Mary was dumbfounded.

'Well?' he demanded.

Mary looked puzzled. O'Connor seemed more concerned than angry.

'Stella did as I asked,' he said. 'Tuesday, she went and had a look at the file you wanted. It contained only the Inspector's report and two witness statements—one from a Samuel Grainger and the other from his wife, Elizabeth. The report didn't say much other than a Daniel Fuller had murdered his stepparents—Joshua and Cissie Fuller. Their bodies were never found, and the Inspector drew the conclusion that the boy had weighed them down and disposed of them in the river.

'So far, so good, you might think!' He snorted under his breath. 'Well, that in the first place should have told me something—two witness statements and an Inspector's report only? For a double murder? Some investigation!' he said, disgustedly. 'Stella managed to copy down the Inspector's statement before she got disturbed. So she thought she'd go back after a while and copy down the witness accounts and be done with it. So she does. And what does she find? The file's gone. Vanished, just like a conjuring trick.'

'Maybe she misfiled it when she put it back?' Mary said.

'She was thinking the same. It was her night for working late, so she goes back later that evening. And there it is, not misfiled, but where it should be. Oh, and by-the-by, it's grown like Topsy. Suddenly, it contains several more witness statements—a vicar, a postman, and who knows who else. From being a thin little file, it's become a fat one. But what takes the cake is that all the *new* statements have been written on *new* stationery. We changed forms a year back and the murder happened three years ago, so Stella's confused. Well, it's too late to do anything, so she leaves with the intention of picking it up again in the morning.

'She gets in early yesterday, so she'd have time to finish copying the stuff, and what does she find? Why, someone's asking questions about the case. Lots of questions. And one of the questions is why Stella is looking at that file. How they knew she was, she don't know. She's like you: pretty good at being sneaky! She tells them what I told her to say in case she's found out: that I asked her to get it, and she did it because it is her job to get things and not ask questions.

'Next thing I know, I'm up before some Major with Inspector Lestrade in tow, and the Major's demanding to know what I want that file for.'

'What did you tell him?' Mary asked.

O'Connor clucked. 'What could I tell him? Don't worry, I kept you out of it. I told him I was thinking about maybe taking the Inspector's exam next year, and I wanted to look at as many unsolved cases as I could to help me with the questions. I don't think he believed me.'

O'Connor threw back his cape in frustration. 'I don't think I'd have believed me, either.'

Mary's eyes bulged. 'Your stripes? Where's your stripes?' she gasped.

The Sergeant's stripes were missing from his sleeves; she could only just make out the ghost of the stitching that said they'd once been there.

'Like I said—I don't think he believed me!'

'Oh no! I'm… I'm… I'm so sorry.' Mary ran her fingers ran along his sleeve, her head drooping. She felt awful. She knew how hard O'Connor worked for his promotion. To lose it because he was doing her a favour made her feel sick to the stomach.

Then she remembered. 'Oh no, what about Stella?'

'She's fine. She was just doing what she was asked, and that's her job, after all,' O'Connor said. 'Anyway, Tuesday, before all this happened and before I knew better, I telegraphed a friend in Gravesend nick. They'll have their own files since it was their case. And what happens? Before I leaves the house this morning, I gets a hand-delivered message from him. It asks what I have I gotten him into? Their files have been impounded and no one is to speak to anyone about it. "No one" he under-lines twice. The Fuller case is off-limits. And he got the distinct impression that the order didn't come from Scotland Yard, but from higher up. And what's higher than the Yard I can only guess.

'So, Finch, like my friend in Gravesend asked—just what have you got me into?'

Mary dragged her eyes away from the policeman's stripeless sleeves and knew she had to tell him the truth.

'Danny Fuller, the accused murderer,' she said, quietly and nervously, 'that's not his name. His real name is… Daniel Finch.'

'Finch?'

'He's my brother.'

'Oh, this gets better and better,' O'Connor whispered to himself.

'It's a long story, but we got separated after our parents died,' Mary said. 'But he's not a murderer, *Serg…* *Consta… Serg…* I mean…' Mary hesitated. 'The Fullers are alive.' And Mary explained how she knew, even showing him the postcard.

'Tell me the rest,' O'Connor said. When she'd finished telling him about Rentham's party and what happened there, the policeman shook his head slowly.

'So, he ain't no murderer, but he's an anarchist instead,' he said. 'Fine distinction, if you ask me.'

'No, he ain't even that,' Mary said, exasperated. 'Danny's no murderer. He's no blackmailer or thief. And he's no anarchist.'

'He just happens to be in the right places at the wrong times,' O'Connor said. Mary's head dropped lower still. 'All right, all right, I apologise, that was uncalled for.'

'If an anarchist planted a bomb at Mr Rentham's party, wouldn't it have gone off on the dance floor, not blown up some gardener's hut?' she said, stubbornly.

'Inspector Gregson doesn't believe that. He thinks the bomb went off prematurely and it was meant to explode in the house. And that's what he's told the papers, and that's what they've printed.'

'No, that's nonsense. Don't they see? Mr Lestrade heard what I said at the time.'

'And he's got his own theories. So what's all this thieving of secret plans? How come we don't know anything about it? All we've been told is some private papers belonging to Rentham was taken and the anarchists would use them to blackmail him.'

Mary gave a deep sigh and felt herself collapsing inward. The police took no notice of her, and treated her like she knew nothing, a child to be ignored.

O'Connor grumbled quietly and looked upwards. 'All right, Finch, I trust you. And after what happened with that file, I know something's up for sure.'

'And I'm being followed,' Mary said. The policeman was startled. Mary explained about the man in the bowler hat.

O'Connor quickly went to the entrance of the alley, scanned both directions of the street and came back.

'Lost him in Swann & Edgar's,' Mary said, proudly.

'Not worried about the someone following you.' The

policeman rubbed his neck. 'I'm worried about the someone who might be following me.'

'But why am I being followed?' Mary asked. O'Connor, though, pointed for Mary to leave the alley at the other end.

'And another thing my friend in Gravesend said in his note: the Graingers have vanished. He went along to speak to them, and they've upped and gone—just like that.'

Mary was worried. Sam Grainger must have realised something was amiss. Did he check and find the postcard missing? The files on the murders were changed, was that because of her visit to him? If that was so, who was Grainger, and was his connections powerful enough to make all this happen? What was he trying to hide, if that was the case? It dawned on her, 'If they've gone, it's a fair bet the Fullers have as well,' she said. 'Someone's trying to keep a secret—'

'And you're in the middle of it,' he said and began to walk away. Then he stopped. 'Then there's that Major. I can't help thinking this has something to do with the Intelligence Service—changing statements, people vanishing, keeping everyone in the dark. It's the sort of dirty work they do.'

'Who are they?' Mary asked.

'Shifty, nasty little… you don't want to know,' and he walked on.

'I'm sorry about your stripes, *Sergeant*,' Mary called to him.

As O'Connor glanced over his shoulders, he grinned at her. 'Easy comes, easy goes as me old mum used to say.'

But Mary knew he was disappointed. Worse still, she was to blame.

16

MYCROFT HOLMES CALLS

WHEN MARY CAME BACK to the pie shop in Baker Street, her shadow had returned. Oddly, one of the official black carriages she saw in Barnes Green was also there.

'But this is excellent.' Mycroft Holmes was seated in the near-empty shop when she entered, his eyes twinkling mischievously. A dish was set before him, a fork was in his hand. 'Ah! Miss Finch, there you are. I was just complimenting Mrs Dibble on this superb creation, and this young lady was telling me all about you.'

'Miss Mary, Miss Mary,' Fortune said, excitedly, 'it's the man from the party.'

Mary walked over slowly. She saw Archie standing behind the door leading to the back of the shop, a worried look on his face. Mycroft Holmes, though, was laughing; he seemed thoroughly at ease.

'If I had known such rare delights existed so near my

brother's residence, I would have partaken without hesitation,' he said. 'I will have to remonstrate with Sherlock for not telling me. Or perhaps he is keeping *you* a secret, Mrs Dibble.' He winked at the old lady.

A wide smile cracked Grandma Dibble's face; she went red and glowed with pride. Mycroft Holmes twirled his fork in a small circle, his eyes closed for a second as he savoured the taste.

'Excellent! Excellent! What do you think, child? Do you not agree?'

Fortune nodded. Her mouth was too full to speak.

'The West Indies,' Mycroft Holmes said. 'You are so far from home, my dear. And such a tragic story. But I hear that Mrs Grady is a first-rate person. I think you are lucky to be in her employ.' He then whispered, 'My dear, I wish to speak to Mary, so perhaps you would be kind enough to share your meal with your new friend. Please forgive my rudeness, but it is important.'

In the corner, the dishevelled figure of Kitty was clutching a glass of milk. A small meal was laid before her that she was intent on eating. Fortune happily joined the young girl, and they instantly started to chat away.

Mary reluctantly joined Mycroft Holmes. She felt decidedly small seated next to such a large man, who seemed to engulf the space around him, even more so when he leant over as if to confide some secret.

'The fare at the Diogenes Club is excellent, Miss Finch, but I have always thought it lacks a good hearty traditional British offering such as this. I must compliment you again.' He gave a polite bow to Grandma Dibble.

'We try our best, sir,' Grandma said, looking happy and pleased, basking under the warmth of the praise.

'Are you not eating?' he asked Mary. She shook her head, suspicious of the man's good cheer. Mycroft Holmes nodded as if to say she was missing something special, then he placed his fork down.

'Sherlock says that I am a man of habit – of course, that is so. He says I run on rails.' Mycroft gave a slight laugh as if remembering a conversation. 'Those rails run from my lodgings in Pall Mall to the Diogenes Club, and thence to Whitehall, where I work. Because I seldom deviate from my route, Sherlock says I lack ambition and energy.' He waved a hand as if to deny the assertion. 'My very presence here disproves his point. At Rentham's, your deductive skills impressed me. I thought we would not meet again—with some disappointment, I must say—then I saw you in Barnes, of all places.'

Mary, who was trying to keep a poker face, glanced up, and was immediately annoyed she did so. She tried to gauge if Mycroft Holmes noticed, but his face was stolidly impassive. When she saw him that day near Boots's house, she had not realised he'd seen her. She should have known better. He was a Holmes, after all. Of course, he'd noticed her.

'What is coincidence?' He plucked at his lips in

contemplation. 'Some say there is no such thing.' He dismissed that explanation with the same wave of the hand as earlier. 'Perhaps it is God's design—a foreordained event. Perhaps. Random things, of course, might be seen as a coincidence. Such as us meeting twice—'

'A third time now,' Mary reminded him and he agreed with a nod of his head.

'Which, of course, might make it a design. Take the case of Boots. A Mr Boots is present at an audacious burglary some nights ago. Lestrade then tells me of a Butler named Boots. Then there is a house in Barnes that belongs to a Mr Boots that the police are interested in. I discover that they are the same person. I further discover that you and he worked in the same household. I, myself, am interested in Mr Boots, and it appears, as are you. So, here we are at the same table. Is it coincidence or design that brings us together? I wonder.'

'Maybe it's just an accident,' Mary blurted. She drummed her fingers nervously and wondered if Mycroft Holmes was making an accusation: that she was involved in what happened. 'I'm curious—I didn't know Mr Holmes had a brother,' she said.

'He does,' he said, dismissively. 'To answer your next question: I hold a small post in the government. I am well known in my somewhat limited circle. I deal in facts. Certain facts come to my attention in the course of my duties. I am incumbent to follow them where they lead. Presently, they lead here.'

'And what facts are we talking about?'

'I believe you know the whereabouts of our Mr Boots.'

His eyes fixed on her intently and Mary shied away from his gaze, not expecting his frankness. She felt that if she looked him in the eye, she would betray some thought, he would read her mind.

'Sorry, Mr Holmes, I don't, and that's the truth.' Mary shook her head.

'If you did, would you tell me?' he asked.

She nodded, a little too quickly, she felt. Then, realising that his presence was making her question her reactions, she became self-conscious.

'He has vanished, and it is imperative he is found,' Mr Holmes said.

'And his friends also? Have they been found?'

'One has, but that you know already.'

'And the other?' Mary asked.

Again, Mycroft Holmes's gaze fell on to Mary, and again her eyes dropped and she found she was looking at the table.

'He is still lost,' he said. 'Perhaps you know of him?'

'Only what I saw,' she said.

'That I was speaking to him, I believe was what you told Mr Rentham.'

'Do you still deny it?' she asked.

'Why should a man in my position speak to an anarchist?'

'I thought he was a thief,' Mary said.

Mycroft Holmes nodded politely. 'Can he not be both?'

Mary shrugged uneasily, not wanting to answer in case her voice betrayed her thoughts. Then she wished she said something as her shrug seemed suggestive of knowledge. And if she said something now… she drummed her fingers nervously.

He was, she could not help noticing, both like and unlike his brother. The penetrating gaze; she did not doubt that, like Sherlock, Mycroft Holmes had a clear-thinking mind that ran on some smooth, unfailing clockwork mechanism behind his quiet unblinking eyes. In the oppressive silence, those eyes steadily roamed her face, taking time to survey her. She felt he was somehow dissecting her thoughts.

Her eyes flitted over to Kitty and back again. *What has the girl come to report?* she wondered. At the same time, she wanted to ask Mycroft his real reason for coming here.

Suddenly, he pushed his chair back. Rising, he turned towards Grandma Dibble.

'Madam,' he said loudly, 'you have my recommendation. The proof is in the eating, and no greater endorsement is needed than that, I assure you. Your servant, madam.'

Grandma Dibble giggled and blushed brightly.

When Mycroft Holmes reached the door, he spoke without turning around.

'It was Napoleon, I believe, who said there is no such thing as accident; it is fate misnamed. I suspect that there is some truth there. Good day, Miss Finch, Miss Dubois.' He glanced over and tipped his hat. 'Kitty… *Short-Pants,* I believe is the sobriquet. One of Wiggins's lot, are you not? My brother's Irregulars. They are well and kept busy with a suitable commission, I trust.'

17

KITTY SHORT-PANTS
BRINGS NEWS

IT SURPRISED Mary how his presence so dominated the shop that when he left, its lack was sorely felt. Even so, the relief that he was gone was palpable. He had been there a good half-hour in total.

Mary wrung her hands and a knot tightened her stomach. Archie told her, Mycroft Holmes said he came to visit his brother. As Sherlock wasn't there, he dropped into the pie shop. He'd lied to Fairchild Rentham, she remembered, when he told him that his brother was away on a case. If he really believed that Sherlock was away, why then was he here?

When she looked across to Fortune, still happily eating and speaking to Kitty, Archie seemed to read her thoughts.

'Fortune mentioned Danny,' Archie said. 'She didn't mean to say anything.'

Mary nodded, understanding how it could have happened. She could imagine the conversation that must have taken place. Mycroft Holmes had an easy way about him, but he was deceptive. That was why he made her nervous. She instinctively understood that he recorded not only what was said to him, but also what was not said. And the reason he'd left was that he found out all he needed. His parting remark to Kitty was not directed at the small girl, but at Mary. He guessed she was searching for Mr Boots and for her brother.

But at least she knew something as well. He did not strike her as someone who did things on the off chance. His purpose for being in Baker Street was a lie.

He asked why a man in his position needed to *speak to an anarchist.* He held a minor position in the government, he said. Again, that seemed to be a lie. The way he carried himself, his mannerisms and assuredness when he spoke to Mr Rentham suggested otherwise. Why *would* a man with a government office, minor or not, speak to an anarchist? Especially when secret plans were going to be stolen and false information given to the police. She wondered just what it was the constabulary were investigating. Anarchists and potential blackmail, it seemed, and not a matter of national security.

But if Mycroft Holmes did know Danny, if they were working together, why was he looking for Mr Boots? Surely Boots and Danny were partners—yet she had a distinct impression that it was Boots Mycroft wanted to find. *He has vanished; it is imperative he is found*, he'd said. Did something go wrong in Barnes, at Boots's house? Was Boots meant to meet Mycroft Holmes there, only for Lestrade to arrive before him? Was that why the distinguished gentleman, who, thanks to the distinctive crest, Mary now suspected to be a German official, was there, too? For Mycroft to hand the plans to?

But Mycroft Holmes a traitor? The thought rattled around her head. It seemed preposterous. Even if he were, who would believe her? If he denied it, they would believe him, and what could she do about that? Especially as it was her brother who stole the plans. Mycroft had all the power; she had none.

'Miss Mary,' Fortune said, 'Mrs Grady wants to know if you are all right. She is worried about you.'

Mary came out of her reverie and smiled as if to say everything was fine. At that moment, Kitty sat back in her chair and pushed away her empty plate and glass, a deeply satisfied look on her face.

'Cor, thanks, missus,' she said to Grandma Dibble. 'I'll tell you, that filled a hole. That bloke was right, that's the best.' She patted her stomach and grinned, then turned to Mary. 'I've got a message for you. But I didn't want to give it when the gent was about.'

'You've found Boots?' Mary said.

'Nah! Sorry.' Kitty shook her head. 'We're still looking. But Wiggins says to tell you he thinks he knows where Bootsie will be.' She pushed a hand into a pocket, pulling out a scrap of paper and handing it to Mary. 'Wiggins said he'll be there at ten this evening. Now let me get this right.' She closed her eyes and set her mouth firm in thought. 'There's to be a meeting of like-minded people who believe in like-minded things about the future of like-minded things. Wiggins said you'd know what he means. But it's a secret meeting, so if you go, you better watch yourself.'

Mary read the note and frowned.

'He said if you wants to hire the Irregulars for the evening, that'll be a tanner each. And if there's any rough and tumble, that'll be another tanner. He's happy if you want to run up a tab. He trusts you since you're friends with Mr Holmes.'

Kitty's face screwed up as she concentrated.

'Now this I have to get right,' she said. 'When you get there, Wiggins told me to say, you're to give a secret knock like this—' She gave five raps on the table—two quick knocks, a space, another two quick ones, a space and a last knock. 'Then say, "*Mr Marx thinks it'll rain tomorrow.*"'

Kitty repeated the instructions.

'And if Bootsie's there,' Kitty said, 'Wiggins says that'll cost you a sovereign. Even so, we'll still be looking for him and that Danny. And when we find their place, that'll be another sovereign.'

Archie was about to say something, but Mary stopped him. She handed over a shiny gold sovereign on account.

Kitty pocketed the coin, withdrew some pennies and went towards Grandma Dibble.

'That was a good feed, missus, and I pays me way,' she said, proudly. 'I ain't no beggar.' She proffered the pennies to the old lady.

Grandma Dibble gave her a motherly look. She reached down and folded the girl's fingers back over the coins.

'That were leftovers,' she said. 'I can't very well serve customers leftovers, can I? And I don't charge for getting rid of them.'

Kitty grinned. 'Cor, thanks, missus. You're the best.'

With that, Kitty left.

'Like-minded things and like-minded people?' Archie asked.

'Anarchists,' was Mary's answer. She then sat down heavily and groaned. Seeing the question on Archie's face, she handed him the scrap of paper. It was a scrawled note of badly formed letters of an address. Archie read it and laughed.

'Limehouse!' Mary said. 'I mean, the meeting couldn't be Hampstead or Mayfair or somewhere posh. It had to be Limehouse.' The last time Mary went in Limehouse was when she tracked down Davey Tupper, and she and Black Bob ended up in the river. She and Archie nearly died that day.

'It's not likely anarchists would hold a meeting in Mayfair,' Archie said.

'Limehouse! But if Boots is there, Danny might be as well.'

'And if he is?'

She was so close to finding someone whom she'd believed lost. It was a bitter blow to find out that he was a criminal. Not a murderer, she reminded herself—the Fullers were alive and living in Wells—but had he become something worse? What happened to him to make him someone who wanted to overthrow the government? She barely understood the word 'revolution' enough to confront someone who believed that way.

Mycroft Holmes, however, still loomed large in her mind. He was at the bottom of this. Though what *this* was, she didn't know. Plotting revolution by selling secrets to a foreign power? Or was it about money, pure and simple greed?

Arms, sir, is where the wealth is these days, Rentham said.

Especially with the situation in Germany, Salter replied.

What was that situation? she wondered. Their growing navy, Mycroft Holmes said.

Who were Danny Fuller and Mycroft Holmes? Revolutionists, or thieves profiting at their country's expense?

✿ 18 ✿

A MEETING IN LIMEHOUSE

As it threatened to be a long night, Archie insisted on a good meal before setting out. Mary, though, picked at her food. She fretted and was anxious to leave, but knew arriving early would not cure her impatience. She would only have to wait there instead of here, and nothing would be gained.

'Grandpa,' Mary said. It was a habit to call Mr Dibble 'Grandpa', even though they weren't related. The old man looked up from his newspaper. 'Someone said something to me about the Intelligence Service. Who are they?'

Grandpa Dibble chuckled.

'Where did you hear that?' he asked.

'From Sergeant—I mean, Constable O'Connor.'

Archie looked at her quizzically, while Grandpa Dibble set his lips meditatively.

'Spies would be a good description of them, I suppose. They are part of the government—not police, mind, but sort of police. The army really is where they best belong. No one knows who they are. That's how they best operate, hidden from sight. If anyone knew them, they'd be of no use anymore. They trade in secrets —stealing or buying them from other countries and making sure none of ours get stolen or bought. They serve the national interest.' He laughed as if what he said amused him. 'All governments have them.'

'All governments?'

'Spies, agents, double agents, even triple agents as well, I suppose.' Grandpa Dibble nodded.

'What's a double agent?'

'Someone who pretends to work for one side, but really works for the other. You need cunning to do that.'

'A false friend, you mean?' Mary said, and again the old man nodded. 'Why do they do it, Grandpa?'

'Some are patriots—you know, love their country, even if it means getting killed for it. Some are greedy. There's lots of money to be made if you have a secret to sell that everyone wants.' Grandpa Dibble chuckled again. 'Why? Are you thinking of becoming one?'

Mary laughed and shook her head.

'But they could be anyone, couldn't they, Grandpa?'

'They could be anyone,' the old man agreed. 'It's dangerous work. Spies gets tortured and executed if they're caught. So, being secretive is how they stay alive.'

Anyone, Mary considered, *even Sherlock Holmes's brother*.

When she and Archie left the pie shop and set out towards Limehouse, Mary noticed that her shadow had emerged from the basement well and was following. She would have to deal with him before they went to the meeting. Since the department stores were closed, she'd have to find another way to lose him.

They spent some time wandering Oxford Street and Soho. They slipped in and out of alleys, moving sharply back again across their path, but still he followed. Before long, she did not need to look; she could feel him somewhere nearby. Occasionally, she saw his reflection in a shop window: a man wearing a bowler hat.

'He's still there.' She despaired. 'Let's see how he likes Seven Dials.' Archie understood and led the way.

By the time they reached Monmouth Street, one of the entrances to Seven Dials, night was falling. They waited, and Mary saw her shadow slip into a doorway and out of sight. Five minutes passed. A group of men were walking towards them, crowding the pavement, and Mary and Archie rested with their backs against a building to allow them to pass. She caught Archie's attention. This was what she was waiting for.

The men passed. Just as they approached the doorway where her shadow was hiding, Mary shouted,

'NOW!' She and Archie dashed away up Monmouth Street. Her shadow emerged from the doorway only to run headlong into the group of men. They got tangled up, pushing, shoving and shouting as he fought his way through them.

The little time this gained allowed Mary and Archie to reach Seven Dials a good deal ahead of her shadow. Seven roads entered the tight circular roadway, and seven roads left it. Once her shadow entered Seven Dials, he wouldn't know which of the six other roads they had taken to leave it.

She decided on a triangle. Turning sharply right, they fled down Mercer Street, and quickly turned right again into Shelton Street. The two sides of the triangle brought them back to where they started. There they turned left and, casually but quickly, walked away from Seven Dials and towards the Strand.

She had lost her shadow.

They found a hansom cab and headed east. She was rather pleased with herself, but her old worries soon returned. Her fingers began drumming against her knee and Archie smiled seeing this. It was one of her habits when she was deep in thought. Even though she was looking out at the street as they trotted along, Mary saw little.

The cab dropped them several streets from the warehouse where the meeting was due to take place. Mary felt that it was best if they arrived on foot. Dismounting the cab in front of a crowd of anarchists might give the wrong impression.

By now, it was fully dark. There were few street lamps in this part of Limehouse and the roads were quiet, the shadows deep. But the clear sky allowed the quarter moon to shine some light to show them the way. Soon, the warehouse was in front of them.

The large brick building wore a weighty frown as it gazed across the road at her. A pair of heavy wooden doors, hinged so they could open outwards into the street, rose almost up to the eaves of the roof. A small door was inset into one of them. They waited across the road.

A few men gave the peculiar knock on the small door, mumbled something, the door opened and they entered. As soon as they did, the small door closed behind them. Mary felt her heart thumping and her breath was sharp. She was ready.

As she started to move, Archie reached out and stopped her.

'A word of advice,' he said. 'It'll be dangerous in there. Don't look at anyone in the eyes; people don't like being looked at. Don't ask questions. I know that'll be a hard one for you, but just talk casually and don't give out any information. If there's a fight—run! Eighty pounds of skin and bones ain't much match against those heavy-weights in there. But if you have to fight—strike low and hard, and then run. I'll look after your back.' He patted his jacket pocket and pulled out a length of lead pipe.

'Just in case.' He slapped the pipe into the palm of his hand and it made a dull thwack.

'You been to one of these meetings before?' she asked.

'I knows some who have,' he said.

Mary took a deep breath. She firmed her mouth and walked to the door. She knocked before her courage failed—two quick taps, a pause, two quick taps, a pause and one more tap.

'What do you want?' A gruff muffled voice came from behind the door.

'Mr Marx thinks it'll rain tomorrow,' Mary said.

'Trust me, it's gonna pour,' the voice said with a laugh. Immediately, the door opened, and she and Archie stepped in. A large man loomed over them. He was grim. His face was battered and scarred, his clothes dirty. He flicked his head as if to say, 'Over there'.

A few oil lamps barely lit the space. It was a cavernous hole. Above them, the ceiling vanished into a yawn of blackness. Wooden crates and boxes were piled on one side, and they too vanished into the darkness the higher they went. Hanging from invisible ropes were pulleys with great metal hooks. Rising up at intervals were thick supporting beams. The rough floor was rutted and covered in straw and sawdust.

In the middle of the warehouse was a group of men, some women and a few children, almost twenty strong. From the midst of their dirty, dishevelled number came a soft murmuring. A man was weaving between them, handing out leaflets and making small talk.

He came to Mary and looked her up and down.

'New? Ain't seen you before,' he said.

Mary flicked her eyes away, remembering Archie's advice.

'Got that right,' Archie mumbled. He took two of the leaflets and gave one to Mary.

'Welcome, Comrades,' the man said, and moved off.

Mary recognised the leaflet—it was the one shown to her by the policeman outside Boots's house at Barnes. In clear bold capitals were the words: The ANARCHIST LEAGUE OF GREAT BRITAIN. There was a crude drawing on one side of the leaflet—a man in a top hat and frock coat, a cigar between his lips, and beside him what looked to be an image of Queen Victoria were being hanged by the neck from gallows.

Archie manoeuvred Mary behind a support beam and into the security of the darkness under it. As her eyes adjusted, Mary noticed that further back and against the walls were others. She peered at the faces, but couldn't see Boots. She wondered if Wiggins got his information right.

There was a commotion ahead. A small, dark-haired man climbed on to a large box. Two gruff and massive fellows flanked him. Their caps were drawn down, hiding their faces, but from under them, their shadowed eyes shone and flicked left and right, their heads moving, constantly scanning the room.

The dark-haired man raised his hands.

'FREEDOM!' he bellowed and immediately everyone fell quiet. A tingle of apprehension prickled the hairs on Mary's skin.

❦ 19 ❦

UNEXPECTED VISITORS

THE SMALL MAN WAS FIERCE. His eyes glowered. He spat his words in a volcanic tirade of curses, oaths and damnation. In occasional quiet moments, he simmered and spoke deeply and sincerely, his voice earnest and pleading. Then he would once more erupt, calling for a fairer and more just society, speaking out against the capitalists, the church, the government and the royalty. Not one was spared his venom.

Soon, those listening murmured approval. They began to cheer each statement, their eyes fixed on him in rapt awe. Even Mary felt herself being carried along with his words. His passion was like a drug she could feel running through her veins, infecting her heart and making it beat faster. She was clenching her fists each time he delivered a charge against the rich and the privileged.

'Why should our children starve?' he asked quietly,

and then his voice rose to a crescendo. 'Why should we toil in factories for a miser's wage? Why should we live in filth? Our young men go jobless; they are thrown away. Our women and children are fit only for the work-house. While those that do nothing, gorge on the fruits of our labour, fill their coffers at our expense, live in luxury you and I can only imagine.'

Mary was taken with his passion. Those listening were so far removed from those who attended Fairchild Rentham's little soirée, they could be on the moon. She was feeling guilty for Mrs Grady, who did attend, even though she knew how charitable to old lady was. Then she felt Archie tugging her arm.

'Over there,' he whispered. 'In the corner. Boots!'

Despite the shadows, there was enough light for her to recognise the profile she knew so well. Boots was standing between two men. They were deep in conversation, ignoring the meeting. Each took a swig from a bottle he'd passed them. It appeared as if they were old friends. But why friends would meet here, at an anarchist rally, Mary could only guess.

She tried to get nearer, but Archie shook his head.

'Not in here,' he said. 'Wait till Boots gets outside, and then we can follow him.'

Archie was right. There were too many people about.

By now, the small vociferous man was haranguing his audience. His face become ugly and menacing. His changed tone caused Mary to glance around nervously. She didn't like what she was hearing.

The crowd grew. Drawn to him by some magnetic attraction, they were listening intently. Some were openly agreeing with him. But something odd was happening.

Several men detached themselves from the throng. Their heads were down and they walked slowly and casually out from the middle of the crowd. She noticed one give the others a furtive look and thought she saw him flick his head towards the door. Two edged away, moving aimlessly towards the entrance to the warehouse.

Mary glanced back towards Boots. He and his friends seemed to have reached some agreement. Boots lifted the bottle into the air, and then brought it down to his mouth and took a swig. He passed it to the man on his right, who did the same. The bottle was passed to the third, and again the same thing happened. Then Boots shook their hands. They were smiling and laughing, patting each other on the back. An arrangement had been made, and Mary knew it wouldn't be a good one.

She turned to Archie, noticing his agitation. His eyes flitted left and right and he chewed his lip. She could feel his nervousness.

'What's wrong?' she asked.

He shook his head and said nothing; his eyes continued to roam the great space inside the warehouse.

The loud man finished speaking. He was sweating profusely. As everyone clapped, he wiped his brow with a dirty handkerchief. Then he began to sing softly. His singing voice was croaky and did not have the power of his speaking one.

> The people's flag is deepest red,
> It shrouded oft our martyred dead,
> And ere their limbs grew stiff and cold,
> Their hearts' blood dyed its every fold...

Odd voices joined him, and before long, many were singing along. Mary recognised the tune, but not the words. Each Christmas for the last several years, she and Emma, a maid she worked with, went to Trafalgar Square to listen to the carollers. As they shared a bag of roasted chestnuts, they would join in when they knew the words. The tune was a German carol, 'O Tannenbaum', that she knew as 'O Christmas Tree'.

The meeting came to an end. As had Boots's. He was laughing with his friends. The bottle was empty. Mary nudged Archie.

'Let's get outside and wait for him,' she said. But even as she spoke, she noticed that behind the loud man, a dark figure slipping across the back of the warehouse. It looked like Danny but she could not be sure. It was too dark to make him out, but she was certain it was her brother. He was going towards Boots.

As he passed a lamp, her heart skipped. It was clearly him. His face, though, was bruised and he sported a black eye. Automatically, she started moving towards him. Archie pulled her back sharply, muttering a low curse. His eyes darted across the warehouse and he cursed again, this time louder.

'What?' Mary asked.

Several things happened at the same moment. A commotion broke out at the entrance of the warehouse. The massive scar-faced doorman was wrestling with two others and they tumbled across the floor. He was being pinned down while a third man was pulling the door open.

Mary's head shot back when Danny gave a frightful yell and sprang at Boots. The two sprawled across the ground, spitting and snarling at each other. Boots's two friends immediately retreated.

Her head spun around again. Through the open door, a rush of dark figures poured into the warehouse. Immediately, hysterical screams erupted from all around, and everyone was pushing and shoving, desperate to get away.

'Coppers! Coppers!' the cry went up.

Helmeted policemen with truncheons raised flew all around. Mixed in amongst them were others without uniforms, shadowy-faced men wearing bowler hats.

'It's a raid,' Archie said and pulled Mary deeper into the gloom.

The small, loud man leapt down from the box. His

bodyguards were fighting with others who sprung out from the crowd towards them.

'We gotta get out,' Archie said.

It was no use trying to reach the small door. More police, including Inspector Gregson, were climbing through it. The Inspector was directing men towards the loud man.

Mary turned to see Danny being flung backwards and crashing into the crates. Boots scrambled to his feet and scampered away into the deepest shadows at the back of the warehouse.

A policeman leapt forward and tackled Danny to the ground, but one of the bowler-hatted men grabbed the policeman and dragged him off. Briefly, the two fought with each other. Danny struggled out from between them and dashed away following Boots.

Mary's heart pounded. Her feet wanted to run, but her mind couldn't decide which way. Archie glanced around, equally lost. There were no windows and Inspector Gregson stood by the doorway they'd entered by. There were plenty of places to hide, but the warehouse would be searched thoroughly.

'This way,' she shouted and pulled Archie along. She ran to where Danny and Boots went. There must be another way out, she reasoned, why else would Boots risked going there. In any case, what was there to lose?

They passed the policeman and the bowler-hatted man who were shouting at each other.

'I had him,' the policeman yelled. 'Didn't you see?'

'I was helping.'

'You wanted the arrest for yourself, that's why you pulled me away.'

'Don't be daft. It was you that messed it up. I had the handcuffs ready.'

The back of the warehouse was black. Mary held out her hands to avoid bumping into anything. Before long, they were in a narrow corridor made up of crates stacked on either side. It was just wide enough to allow passage through in a single file. Ahead, she saw the dull rectangle of an open doorway.

When they reached it, Mary heard the thud of approaching footsteps and shouts of '*Get them!*' coming from behind.

20

THE CHASE

THEY BURST out of the warehouse into a stinking back alley that led in three directions—ahead, to the left or to the right. Mary could just hear the sounds of running feet in the distance. They echoed off the surrounding walls, and she could not tell from which direction they came.

'This river's this way,' Archie shouted.

'I ain't going there,' and Mary rushed forward instead. She was still haunted by her memories of the Thames at Limehouse.

The cobblestones were greasy and Mary slipped, skidded and tumbled. Archie roughly pulled her up. Behind them, Inspector Gregson exited the warehouse. Suddenly, he too tumbled. His hands shot out to break his fall as he crashed. The push of policemen behind him fell over his prone body and landed in a heap around him. Mary caught sight of Kitty hiding just behind the doorway from which they exited. The small girl gave a squeal of triumph and dashed away, quickly disappearing into the darkness. But the Inspector had seen her.

'Kitty Short-Pants,' Gregson shouted. 'Wait till I catch you!'

Like Kitty, Mary and Archie did not linger. They zigzagged through small, dark streets, all the while desperately trying to keep to the shadows so they could not be recognised. Her breath rasped in her throat. Her heart pounded as if trying to escape her chest. Neither she nor Archie spoke a word, all their energies were spent on running. Behind her, she could hear their pursuers ordering them to stop and surrender.

The alleyway opened up into a narrow empty street. Mary quickly looked in each direction and went to the left. They passed a small passage and Archie tugged her inside. They ran to the other end and out into a wider street. The street was better lit, and there were several dark entrances along it to suggest passageways and alleys.

Mary despaired. How long could they keep running? Their pursuers were determined. She could hear the thudding of their footsteps echoing off walls close by.

Ahead of them came the rowdy noise of singing from a public house. Mary sprinted to the door and they ducked inside the brightly lit and smoky room just as a number of policemen bundled into the street behind them. Their sudden entrance caused several customers to look up, but the singing did not stop and the piano player crashed out his tune.

Mary was panting hard; her face was wet with perspiration. She glanced around nervously. Archie was twisting his way through the crowd to go deeper into the pub when Mary stopped him. She grabbed an empty glass from a table and pushed it into his hand.

'Trust me,' she said.

To Archie's surprise, Mary started dragging him back towards the door and the street where the police were. He dug his heels in.

'You gone mad?' he spluttered.

She pulled his arm hard, and they exited the pub in a rush, almost colliding with the three constables about to enter. Gregson wasn't amongst them. She knew the chase would be too hard for him.

'Don't give me any of your lip, Benny,' Mary shouted to Archie. 'Mum's fed up with your drinking. Why is it me that has to come and get you every time? I've got to be up early tomorrow. If I'm late again, I'll get the shove.' She clouted Archie around the head. 'And you lot can get out of my bleedin' way,' she snarled to the policemen. 'Go on, make yourselves useful and give them back this.' She snatched the glass from Archie and shoved it into one of their hands. 'You lazy, good-for-nothing sot, Benny. You're no brother of mine—'

'That's the way, little sister,' one of the policemen said, cheerfully. 'Give him what for.'

'And you can bleedin' shut it, too,' she bellowed at him. The policeman burst out laughing. Archie's stuttering and stammering caused the other two to laugh as well.

Once the constables entered the pub, Mary and Archie moved swiftly away. She knew the constables would spend many fruitless minutes inside, before assuming those they were chasing left via the back door. Deep down, she also knew none of the drinkers would say anything about a girl and her 'brother' who come in and left the pub on seeing the constabulary at the door.

A wide smirk spread across Mary's face as they turned into another street. Archie, though, just shook his head in disbelief.

'I wish you'd tell me next time you have a brainwave like that,' he said with relief, rubbing his head. 'And that clout hurt! Come on, let's find Danny and Boots.' He started walking briskly, but Mary pulled him back.

'It's no use,' she said. 'They probably went by the river or the opposite way. They're long gone. And slow down. We've lost the coppers. If we're casual, no one will suspect anything.'

Now that they were beyond suspicion, or so she assumed, Mary led Archie back to the warehouse. A small crowd gathered to witness the commotion, and Mary and Archie edged nearer to stand just behind a black hansom.

A row of carriages with bars pulled up on the road. A

mess of policemen was escorting various people away from the warehouse. Many were being arrested and placed in the back of the carriages. Few, it seemed, were allowed to go free. The loud man was thrown into one. He glared and spat and, grasping the bars, pulled and beat them angrily. Mingling amongst the mess were the bowler-hatted men.

Inspector Gregson, a little dusty and slightly the worse for wear from his tumble, was speaking to a tall, lean gentleman with a military bearing. Like many present, the gentleman wore a bowler hat, and he carried a rolled-up umbrella. He was resting both hands on the handle and constantly tapped the point of the umbrella on the cobbles like he was sending out a message in Morse code.

When the Inspector finished speaking, the gentleman shook his head and said something that caused Gregson to look vexed. The gentleman then walked to the black hansom that Mary and Archie were standing behind.

A familiar voice spoke to him.

'Well, Major Carshaw?' Mycroft Holmes demanded.

'It was a close thing—apparently, someone tripped the good Inspector. Mercury escaped,' the Major said, smoothing his thin moustache with a finger. 'The Painter, however, is a different matter. It is as you suspect. The night has not been wasted; we have Mad Murdoch at least.' He nodded towards the carriage containing the loud man. 'However, I had to put Gregson right, and he is not best pleased. He wanted to charge him with being an anarchist and with incitement to riot.'

'No, no, that won't do,' Mycroft Holmes said, disgruntled.

'I agree. We have settled on common assault. Murdoch may have his day in court, but it will be in the local assizes and not the Old Bailey. His anarchist views will not be heard and made known. I think he was rather looking forward to the publicity of a big trial.'

'Good, good,' Mycroft Holmes said. 'That won't happen with an assault charge. He will disappear to some provincial jail for several years and be forgotten. The less publicity the anarchists get, the better.'

'We are running out of time,' the Major said. 'The *Wilhelm* sails on Saturday. We may have to make other arrangements.'

'Major, that would be most inconvenient.'

'It would have been *convenient* if your man told us there was a back door to this place.'

'It would have been appropriate to have checked.'

The Major bit his lip and tapped the end of his umbrella several times on the cobbles in frustration.

'What would you have me do with those arrested?' The Major nodded to the men and women who had been in the meeting and were now in custody.

'Nothing. Take their details and let them go. I suspect there is not a revolutionary amongst them. If we start charging too many, it will only draw suspicious eyes.'

'And that would defeat the exercise.' Major Carshaw looked skywards and tightened his lips. *'A domestic incident occurred in Limehouse, occasioning a large commotion.'* He said it airily, as if reading a story in tomorrow's newspaper—and that a story which would only appear somewhere deep inside the edition. 'That will not please the good Inspector.'

'Then perhaps we ought to throw him a bone,' Mycroft Holmes said, 'and keep a few of these people arrested for a day or so.'

Nodding, the Major took a deep breath and walked back across the street to speak to Inspector Gregson. At the same moment, the black hansom moved off.

21

KITTY HAS MORE NEWS

'WHAT WAS ALL THAT ABOUT?' Archie asked.

Mary did not reply. She began to move away from the warehouse, heading towards a main road from which they could find a hansom to take them home. Her mind was tired and she was hungry. It was late and she felt as if she was swimming in treacle. Nevertheless, she too was wondering what was going on.

Once they found a cab, she slumped down and closed her eyes. So, that was the Major the policeman mentioned back in Barnes, the one Mycroft Holmes brought in to investigate. Lestrade and Gregson might be Inspectors, but Major Carshaw seemed to be in charge. And Mycroft Holmes, it appeared, was in charge of him.

She placed her head against Archie's shoulder and dozed. A sudden bump of the wheels awoke her with a start. She was surprised; they were in Baker Street, and she must have slept the whole journey.

'Wakey-wakey!' Archie whispered.

Mary yawned and rubbed her eyes. It was gone midnight. The street was dark, but the lights were still on in number 221B. For a full minute, Mary gazed up at Sherlock Holmes's flat until she realised that Archie had opened the door to the pie shop and was waiting patiently. Once inside, she sat down at one of the tables and he vanished. Several minutes later, he returned carrying a tray of cold leftovers, bread and a glass of milk.

Mary ate in silence until the tray was cleared. Then she sat back.

'Remember me telling you about that house that blew up in Greek Street in February?' she said wearily.

'When you were working for the Grimwigs? Gas explosion, wasn't it?'

'I think it was a bomb,' Mary said. 'Same with the one that blew up in Kilburn, and the one that went up in the East End a few days ago. The papers were all writing about how anarchists were responsible, and then the next day they were all saying it was gas. Mr Holmes and that Major must have convinced the press that they were all accidents. It's what he was saying back there.'

'The less publicity the anarchists have, the better,' Archie remembered. 'They're keeping it under wraps.'

'That's their game. That Major Carshaw ain't part of

the police. He's with some other force, that Intelligence Service, O'Connor spoke about, I'd warrant a guess. O'Connor said they can make things happen—change witness statements, make people vanish.'

'And make sure Mad Murdoch is charged with common assault, not incitement to riot,' Archie added.

'That takes a bit of power.'

'Sherlock Holmes's brother, you mean.'

'He ain't no small cog in government, no matter what he says.' Mary arose and wandered lazily across to the window. She peered out into the darkness. A drift of smoke came from the basement well of the house across the street. She saw the orange-red glow of the tip of a cigarette. Her shadow was back.

'Did you see the other men with the coppers, the ones in the bowler hats?' Mary huffed and nodded to the man in the shadows. 'I think Mycroft Holmes is as dodgy as they come. But I don't understand why. He's got power, so maybe he wants money as well. He knows Danny, I know that for sure. He knew those plans were going to be stolen. He didn't know Danny was my brother, though, but he's figured that out.'

'How so?' Archie asked.

'He must have started to figure it out at Mr Rentham's place. He saw my chain and knew it meant something. And if he's working with Danny, he might have remembered, he wore one the same.' She pointed with her chin to the basement well. 'And because of him over there.'

Archie gave a slight laugh, remembering their trick at Seven Dials.

'I bet he ain't pleased.'

'I thought he was a policeman, but he ain't. He's one of that Major Carshaw's men, and I reckon that means Mycroft Holmes. He's had me spied on ever since we came back from Gravesend.'

'Sam Grainger alerted him, you mean?'

Mary nodded. 'I bet that's what Sam Grainger was doing in the post office, sending the Major or Mr Holmes a telegram. Then when they found out O'Connor looked at the file on the Fullers, they would have known for sure we were on to their game. That's why the statements were changed and added to, to make it look like a thorough investigation had taken place.'

'But if the Fullers aren't dead—'

'Then why keep it a secret?' she asked. 'For some reason, it is important that they should. That's why they changed the statements. But something went wrong. Something Mr Holmes didn't foresee. And he's running out of time. That German gunboat… whatever is going on has something to do with that.'

A quizzical look came on to Archie's face.

'You know what went wrong?' he asked.

'I think so,' Mary said. 'Did you see how Danny and Boots were fighting? If they were partners, why would they fight? Danny was sporting some bruises; he didn't have them when I saw him at that party. I think they had a falling out, and Boots has the plans.'

'Which means he's double-crossed Danny and Mr Holmes—'

'And that's why they have to find him.'

She came and sat down again, resting her head in the palms of her hands, her elbows on the table.

'Mary, you all right?' Archie asked.

'This is not just about money, Archie,' she said wearily. 'What if Mycroft Holmes is a double agent and it's the Germans he's really working for?' She shook her head; it didn't seem possible. But even so, it didn't seem ridiculous, either. She could not help thinking that he was at the centre of all of this. But she could not very well go and tell Inspector Lestrade; he would not believe her. 'Mr Holmes knows the Fullers are alive. But he wants everyone to believe they're dead and Danny is a murderer.'

Archie sat down and took a deep breath. 'Why?' he asked simply.

'To get Danny to do his bidding by making him think he's killed them? Maybe.'

It makes some sense, Mary thought. If Danny believed he was responsible for the Fullers' murders, then he'd do anything Mr Holmes wanted to keep himself from the gallows. She folded her arms on the table and lowered her head against them, crying softly.

'What's Danny got himself into, Archie?' she sniffled. 'Mr Holmes must have something on him to make him steal secrets. I wish Danny was here and none of this had happened. None of this is fair. He's being used.' She rubbed her eyes against her sleeves to clear the tears away. 'And when it all tips up, who'll get the blame? Not Mr Holmes or that Major, that's for sure. They'll be acting all proper, like butter wouldn't melt in their mouths.'

She clearly saw an outcome she dreaded: Danny getting caught, and what would happen then? What happens to traitors?

'But if I can get the plans from Boots,' Mary said, 'I might be able to use them as leverage to make them to leave Danny alone, and maybe clear his name. That's the best I can think of at the moment. I don't know what else to do.'

There was a series of sharp, urgent raps on the door. When Archie opened it, Kitty slipped in swiftly and went to crouch under a table by the window. She peeped out and glanced along both sides of the street. When she was satisfied, she came nearer to Mary.

'That Gregson's after me,' she said in a hoarse whisper. 'He thinks I tripped him up at that warehouse.' She looked appalled. 'It was him that tripped over me, it was. How was I to know he'd do that? If I knew he'd do that, I'd have been elsewhere, I would have.'

Mary wanted to hug the girl for her timely intervention, but Kitty shied away.

'Here, mister,' she said to Archie. 'Can I hole up here till tomorrow? I'll leave then, promise. The heat'll be off by then, I reckon.'

Archie was about to say yes, but Kitty turned brightly to Mary.

'Here, miss! After Mr Gregson had his accident, I saw Bootsie. I followed him,' she said proudly with a wide smirk across her face. 'He got a hansom and I clung on to the back. Look at me mitts! They're red-raw from holding on.' She showed Mary her fingers. 'It dropped him near Regent's Park, but I couldn't see where he went. I had a bit of bother with the cabbie. He spotted me, you see, and I had to leg it. I reckon that's worth sixpence, ain't it, miss?'

'Where in Regent's Park?' Mary asked.

'Up the road a bit, not far from Baker Street station.'

'Of course!' Mary shouted. 'Why didn't I think of it? That's worth a sovereign, Kitty. Archie, I know where Boots is. Kitty, when you see Wiggins tomorrow, tell him the hunt's off and I want him to do something for me.'

She gave the girl a shiny gold coin. Kitty's face flushed as she clutched her prize. She breathed on it and gave it a polish on her blouse, and then held it up, the gold reflecting against her cheeks.

'Cor, miss, you're the best, you are,' she said.

❦ 22 ❦

THE STAKE-OUT

KITTY LEFT EARLY the next morning after a large breakfast, which she ate voraciously. It occurred to Mary that the little girl might not eat again that day, and the same thought must have occurred to Grandma Dibble. As Kitty left, Grandma gave her a wink and passed her a half loaf of bread and a not so small wedge of cheese wrapped in brown paper.

At mid-morning, Mary and Archie left.

It surprised Mary how easily she lost her shadow. He was clearly following when they went into the Marshall & Snelgrove department store; in fact, and to her surprise, he made little attempt to hide. When they exited from one of the side doors, he had gone. The Intelligence Service's lack of vigilance confused her, she had expected it to be more difficult this time, especially after her trick at Seven Dials.

Before long, they were in Regent's Park. Crossing its open ground gave Mary a chance to confirm they were not being followed. Some people lounged on the grass and under the trees; nannies with perambulators and their charges wandered lazily along the paths; a young woman with a severe face, carrying an artist's sketchpad, her young man in tow, passed them; no one looked suspicious. Soon, Mary was gazing up at the Grimwigs' old house. Quietly, she and Archie slipped away and hid behind some bushes, and waited.

The house, where Boots was the Butler and Mary a maid, had been empty and boarded up since her former employers, the Grimwigs, left London. She wondered why she had not considered it earlier, that after Boots's house was raided, he would hide here. But now, standing in front of it, she understood. The house harboured bad memories. When she left it to work for Mrs Grady, she'd thought she would never see it again, at least not this closely, nor go inside, as she intended to do.

'Penny for your thoughts,' Archie said.

Mary sighed and shook her head. 'Just thinking back to when I first came here and how lucky I've been since.' She hunkered down. It would be a long wait. 'Grandma took me around the back and into the kitchen,' Mary said. 'I was so afraid, I clutched Grandma's hand so tightly, she must have thought I'd never let go. I wasn't even eleven yet, and this place was so different from the one before.'

'Mrs Fortesque. That old cow.' Archie reminded Mary of how she'd once described the lady she'd worked for before the Grimwigs.

'That first day,' Mary smirked with glee, 'Cook glared at me. God! How she frightened me. I wanted to run away there and then; I was terrified of her. Then she started laughing and pinched my cheeks. She and Emma were having me on. Even Grandma was in on it. Oh, how they laughed! The look on my face must have been priceless.

"I had you going there, didn't I? You should have seen how your little lips trembled," Cook kept on saying. I was so relieved; I thought it was the best day of my life until Boots walked in. I can still remember how he scared me. I'd never heard a voice that rough before.

' *"I'm Mr Boots."* ' She imitated his voice. ' *"I am the Butler. You'll address me as Mr Boots and your employer as Mr Grimwig or the master. Do as you're told, do it well, do it right and we will get on like a house on fire. But take care to do as you're told, do it well and do it right, otherwise, you and me will have words."* The room became ever so quiet afterwards. I'll never forget that.'

Mary glanced up and scanned the windows at the very top of the house. She counted them until her eyes settled on one. That was her little attic room gazing out across the park, the one she'd so loved.

Mary bowed her head and forced thoughts of the past from her mind. Things were coming to a head, she felt it keenly now she knew where Boots was hiding. The only thing that mattered was the present and what that would mean for the future.

'Look,' Archie said. 'It's Wiggins.'

The boy was running along the path. Every now and then, he'd peer behind some bushes, looking for them. He just passed the artist, who was busy sketching with her young man still beside her, when he saw Archie waving.

Wiggins scampered over. Still panting, he crouched beside Mary.

'Found you,' he said. 'Kitty gave me your message. I've got the lads positioned all around the roads to the house like you asked. If Boots comes or goes and you miss him, we won't. As soon as we see anything, we'll get back to you. You sure he's in there?'

'He's there all right.' Mary's eyes flicked up and across to one side of the building. A thin line of blue-grey smoke was drifting out from a chimney. 'He's making luncheon, no doubt. And the drawing room window looks like it's been busted.'

Mary pointed to a window behind some overgrown bushes where the pane was broken.

'You expecting trouble?' Wiggins asked. He wore a mischievous look on his face as if it was something he was relishing.

'I'm not sure,' Mary said. The last thing she wanted was trouble. Last night's escapades were still fresh in her mind. 'If Boots leaves, I want you to follow him. But if he's carrying a large portfolio, like what artists carry, then get to me quick. Maybe then there'll be some trouble. But if he ain't, then me and Archie will go in and see if we can find it. If we have to search, it might take us a while. It's a big house. So make sure you let us know if he returns.'

They agreed on a signal. Wiggins would hoot like an owl. He gave them a demonstration.

'Bleedin' queer owl,' Archie grinned, 'if he's up and about, hooting during the daytime.'

Wiggins grinned back. 'You sure he's in there alone?' he asked.

'I reckon,' Mary said, knowing Boots. 'The two men he was talking to at the warehouse got arrested. He was probably striking up some deal with them. Now they ain't here, I'm guessing he's alone, all right.'

'Well, we're here if there's to be a tumble,' Wiggins said and rubbed his hands together in glee. 'Just whistle and we'll come.'

'Remember, he's dangerous,' Mary said. 'He tried to kill Archie and me once, and almost succeeded. So don't go underestimating him.'

'Oh, don't worry about us. We're used to trouble,' Wiggins said and winked.

When he left, Mary squatted down once again. It would be a long day and she brought sandwiches, drink and several newspapers. If they were still there when the park closed, they might have to find another place to wait.

'We're going to steal the plans back, Archie,' she said. She gritted her teeth and scowled. 'Then I'm going to use them to force Mr Holmes to release Danny, get him to tell the truth about the Fullers and make this all right again. I don't know how I'm going to do it, only that I am going to do it. Just you see.'

✖ 23 ✖

A SURPRISE MEETING

THEIR WAITING DRAGGED ON, endlessly it seemed, and Mary yawned widely. The day that started out hot became overcast and desperately humid as thick, heavy clouds gathered. Then the sky reddened as night approached. Slowly, the park emptied until only some evening walkers were about.

The young lady was still sketching; her man had left many hours ago. As the light failed, she also left. In all that time, the Grimwigs' boarded-up house remained silent. No one came and no one went. At one point, Mary caught sight of a face peering from behind an upstairs window. It was Boots, scanning the streets. On several occasions, Mary succumbed to the sapping heat and dozed dreamlessly. When she wasn't sleeping, it was Archie's turn to close his eyes.

In the murky light before night fell, Mary watched the

glow of a candle moving through the darkened ground floor of the house, past one window and then the next. When it reached the broken drawing room window, it stopped and vanished as it was extinguished. She saw a gleam of light as the window was pushed up and open, and watched a shadowy figure ease itself out.

She nudged Archie awake. Boots slipped across the wide front lawn, through the gate and along the pavement. He wasn't carrying anything.

Mary waited, hoping that Boots would not return soon. But if he did, at least the hoot of an owl would not seem out of place now that it was night. Fifteen minutes passed before she decided it was safe to carry out her plan and they crept forward. They passed through the gate and crossed the overgrown and unkempt lawn to the broken window, easing through.

The house was quiet and dark. Archie lit the lantern he carried. He kept the wick low, but held the lantern high.

Ghostly white dust covers encased the furniture that dotted the room. A few tables, however, had the covers thrown back. Some plates, glasses and cutlery were collected at the edge of one. The dusty parquet floor gleamed dully. From the ceiling, the chandelier hung, sparkling in the lamplight. The room smelt musty: an unlived-in, abandoned smell.

'Where do we start?' Archie whispered.

Mary took a deep breath. She looked around. The

house was vast. But even so, it seemed more than likely Boots would have hidden the portfolio somewhere on the ground floor. At least, that was where she decided to start looking.

'What's that noise?' Archie asked. 'Rats?' He shielded the light and the drawing room went black.

From somewhere ahead came a rasping sound. It was sharp and clear in the silent house, sounding like claws scratching and scratching, scraping and picking. The odd sound was coming from the library beyond the morning room where the Grimwigs once took breakfast.

Archie adjusted the lamp until it emitted a narrow beam that illuminated only the floor immediately in front of them. They crept forward.

Was it her imagination? The noise was getting louder.

Mr Boots certainly wasn't in the house, and the house had been empty for a good five months, so perhaps it was rats after all. With no one living there, the pests were at liberty to roam wherever they wanted. Or perhaps a bird had fallen down the chimney and was dying behind the hearth. Even so, Mary shivered. She glanced at Archie and swallowed her fears, glad he was with her.

Archie brushed against a table. Something dislodged. He reached to grab it, missed, and a metal salver clattered against the floor. In the silent house, it sounded as if someone had rung a gong. Archie clenched his teeth and screwed up his eyes in annoyance. Mary glared at him.

The noise ahead of them stopped. The clatter of the

salver must have scared away the rats or frightened the trapped bird.

The door to the library was ajar. Archie went in first. He was clutching the length of lead pipe he had shown Mary at the warehouse meeting, but he looked nervous—no more so than she. He turned the wick higher.

The library was as Mary remembered: the shelves still crowded with the books the Grimwigs never read. But all the dust covers were removed from the furniture. A settee that belonged in the drawing room was dragged inside. Some blankets and a pillow confirmed her suspicions: Boots slept here.

Curiously, a window behind a set of heavy floor-length drapes was wide open. In one corner of the room was a large cast-iron safe that belonged to Mr Grimwig. It was four feet high, almost three feet wide and just as deep. Even more curious was the variety of objects on the floor around it—small tools, screwdrivers, a hammer and other sharp implements.

Mary crouched beside the iron safe and picked up a few of the strange objects and looked at them quizzically. A thin metal rod was protruding from the keyhole on the door. Why was Boots trying to break into Grimwig's old safe? Surely, he had the key. Grimwig trusted him implicitly.

A voice hissed from behind the curtains, 'What're you doing here, Midge?'

She started and arose sharply in panic, her heart

banging in her chest. At the same moment, Archie spun around, the lead pipe raised. He tensed, ready to fall on the person who just spoke.

A hot flush washed over Mary and she choked loudly. No one called her 'Midge' for going on ten years. Her parents were the last ones; them and…

'Danny?' she gasped.

Peering around the side of the curtains was the face of the young man she saw talking to Mycroft Holmes at the party a few days ago; the same face she'd seen in the newspaper; the one she'd glimpsed as they struggled in the garden of Fairchild Rentham's house; the same one as at the meeting in Limehouse. She saw her brother's bruised and frightened face looking at her.

'Damn it, Midge, what are you doing here?' Daniel Finch's harsh, urgent whisper sounded like a shout in the quiet house.

'Danny…?' Mary stammered. 'I thought… I thought… I…' She was almost crying. Her legs wobbled as she struggled to remain calm while reeling in shock. A lump formed in her throat as she gasped for breath. Then suddenly, a huge smile spread across her face and she rushed forward.

'Archie, it's Danny!' she shouted.

Archie flicked his eyes to the ceiling. 'Tell it a little louder, maybe,' he moaned.

Mary was speechless. All she could do was hug Danny and whimper back her tears. It was a moment she dreamed about for so many years. Once it seemed as if it would never happen. Now all her years of waiting came out in the hug she gave her brother. She could barely contain herself. She wanted to jump and run and shout. There was so much she wanted to tell him; she did not know where to begin.

Daniel Finch held his sister tightly.

'I've come to help,' Mary said, happily.

'Help?' Danny replied. 'What have you done, Midge?' Concern etched his voice. He too seemed lost for words. 'I thought you were dead,' he said after a minute. 'Joshua told me you died in Liverpool. But when I saw the locket… I knew it was you…'

'I know, Danny.' Mary's face blossomed red and she beamed back at him. 'We've come to get the plans and clear your name.'

She felt Danny stiffen and saw his smile fall away and the worry in his face that replaced it.

'Plans?' he said, cautiously.

'The ones you and Boots stole from Mr Rentham.'

Danny pushed her away to arm's length. He looked confused.

'Oh no, Midge!' he said. 'How did you know? Who've you told? Midge, who've you been talking to?'

He was breathing heavily and Mary felt his hands tighten around her arms. She winced and instantly Danny released her. She could sense his fear. He was speaking like Mr Grainger had to Bessie.

'Danny,' she said, hesitantly. 'What's going on?'

Now she saw the dread in his eyes.

'I can't tell you,' he said. 'It's for your own good. Now tell me, what have you done, Midge?'

'D-d-done? B-but I don't understand,' Mary garbled. 'I've come to help you clear your name. Danny, the Fullers are alive. I can prove it. Was that how Mr Holmes made you steal the plans? By threatening to tell the police that you killed them? Don't you see? He can't, because they're not dead. All we have to do is find them, and I know where they are. And I know you ain't an anarchist, Danny, or a traitor; I just know it. And… and…'

She fell silent. Daniel Finch looked as if he had been struck a blow. The colour washed out of his face. He was shaking his head slowly.

'Oh, Midge,' he said. He pulled her close to him and hugged her tightly, but now she knew his tenderness was concern, not relief.

24

BOOTS AND THE TRAITOR

'YOU DON'T UNDERSTAND what you've got yourself involved in,' Daniel Finch said. 'You must leave and let me deal with this.'

'But what's going on?' Mary asked.

He pushed her away and rubbed his neck in anguish.

'I can't tell you. It's best if you don't know, for your own sake.' He glanced at Archie, as if asking who he was.

Archie bowed. 'Archibald Socrates Dibble,' he announced. 'Look, lovely family reunion and all that, but if we hang about telling stories, Boots will be listening in on them as well.'

'You've got to get her away,' Danny said. 'Midge, you've got to go with him.'

Mary pouted, shook her head and stood her ground.

'You're wasting your breath, mate,' Archie said. 'You

don't know your sister. She ain't budging. So come on, let's find those plans and get out. This place troubles me.' He nodded to the safe. 'If they're in there, then we're done. I ain't no cracksman. And the three of us sure ain't gonna lug that out of here. It probably weighs a ton.'

'Damn it!' Danny gave a sigh of resignation. 'You were always awkward.' Mary raised her head high as if it were a compliment. 'Turn that lamp up a bit,' he said to Archie and knelt beside the safe.

'Are you trying to tell me–'

Danny shot him a look and Archie did as he was asked.

Danny intertwined his fingers and cracked his knuckles. He gathered together the jemmy and a dozen long pieces of metal with sharpened hooks at the end that looked like medical devices. Some were twisted and ridged, but each was subtly different. In a bag beside him, Mary noticed a stethoscope. He exhaled and inhaled deeply. He was ready.

'All right you two,' he said. 'Keep quiet until I'm done. I need to concentrate.'

Danny probed the lock with the various instruments. He picked one metal rod up, and then another, and Mary realised the clicking noise she'd heard earlier was the sound of Danny trying to open the safe. He seemed to know what he was doing, and she wondered where he had learned such a thing.

Soon he had three of the probes inside the keyhole of

the safe, and he grasped each in such a way as to keep them apart yet together. His face was damp with sweat. But time was pressing. Almost an hour had gone since Boots left. Archie kept anxiously looking over his shoulders. He fidgeted nervously, and several times Danny reminded him to keep the light steady.

'We need to hurry,' Archie whispered.

'A Tann's Defiance Safe and Lock is problem enough without you yapping,' Danny said with a glare. 'It would have been easier if it was a combination lock—those I can do in my sleep.'

Mary's mind flew back to Fairchild Rentham's house. That safe had been a combination lock, so why did Danny use explosives to open it? So many odd things were happening.

'Come on, come on,' Danny gasped to himself. He twisted his hand, straining with the effort, holding each of the instruments apart, his face colouring red. He was breathing hard and more beads of sweat wetted his forehead. Bracing his shoulders against the safe, he suddenly turned his hand and there was a sharp click.

'Got it!' He exhaled loudly and fell backwards with the effort. A wide smirk of triumph broke over his face as he looked up at them and pulled the door open.

'Hurry, get the plans and let's go,' Archie whispered.

The safe contained a large portfolio with a black leather cover. There was a look of relief on Danny's face as he took it out. Then he seemed to remember Mary and turned towards her.

'Midge, I can't explain…' There was hesitation in his voice, the meaning of which Archie understood.

'He's going to give the plans to the Germans,' he said, drily.

'Danny?' Mary said.

'He's a traitor after all.'

'Don't say that. My brother's not a traitor,' Mary yelled at Archie. 'Tell him you're not, Danny.'

'Those plans are secret,' Archie said. 'If they fall into the wrong hands—'

'You can't do that, Danny. I can help. If you're in trouble with Mr Holmes, we can sort it out together. Mrs Grady will help us as well. She's got money and she'll hire a good lawyer…'

Her voice faded to nothing when she saw the determination in her brother's face.

'Midge,' Danny said in despair, 'I need to do this. Please don't try to stop me, because I can't explain. It's far too dangerous. And it's important. That's all you need to know. The Germans have got to get this.'

'But why?' Mary pleaded. 'Please, Danny, tell me and let me help. Whatever it is, we can fix it, I'm sure of it.'

She despaired. There was something in her brother's eyes she could not decipher. A resolve, some sort of purpose. The very thought he would betray his country made her nauseous. He wasn't an anarchist; of that she was certain. But a traitor? Her mind swirled in confusion.

He turned to Archie. 'Don't try to stop me. I don't want a fight. It's going to the Germans, and that's that. It has to, and I have to do it.'

Mary grasped his arms and dragged him around. She desperately wanted to understand as she struggled to stop herself crying. So many questions inhabited her clouded mind, she struggled where to start.

'What has Mr Holmes got on you, Danny?' As she asked this, she became aware of the urgent hooting of an owl. Suddenly, the curtains of the open window parted and Wiggins pushed his head through.

'You lot deaf or what?' he hissed. 'You're lucky I found you. I've been hooting for bleedin' hours! Come on, this way.' The boy retreated in fear.

Archie swore. 'We've gotta go!'

He pushed Mary and Danny towards the window. As they reached it, the gravelly voice of Boots boomed from behind them.

'How touching.'

Mary's eyes slewed back in horror. The Butler was standing in the doorway, pointing a pistol at them. How long he had been there, she didn't know. His face was dark with menace.

'Mary *bloody* Finch,' he said. 'I should have known you'd be mixed up with this. So, the anarchist is your brother! If I'd known that before…' he snarled gruffly.

'You got lucky I didn't, Danny, otherwise you'd be floating down the Thames.'

'You tried that already,' Danny said, stepping in front of Mary to shield her.

'Yes, and it was a shame the coppers didn't do a good enough job back at my house.'

'So it was you that informed on us.'

'They missed you by minutes, I'd guess. Well, at least they got one.'

Boots flicked the gun to warn Archie to back away and put down the pipe he was carrying. He glanced at the safe.

'A cracksman as well as a bomb maker! I am impressed. Those anarchists taught you good. Throw it!' he said gruffly and nodded at the portfolio. Danny held it out for Boots to come and get it. The Butler smiled. 'Throw it!' he whispered.

Danny swung the portfolio over and Boots picked it up. His eyes never left Danny Finch.

'Don't look so surprised,' Boots said to him. 'This is business—more pleasurable business since your sister interfered in my last one. You caused me an awful lot of trouble and money, Mary. I should have ignored Grimwigs' qualms that night of the robbery and wrung the information out of you.' His lips curled in utter disgust at the memory of those days. He turned his attention back to her brother. 'I can't say I ever shared your beliefs. But, I think you knew that.'

'We knew you were never really one of us,' Danny said.

'But I had the connections to get the dynamite and the other stuff you needed. You should have listened to me. Ironic, isn't it? That thing you want to get rid of, money, is what your cause needs the most,' Boots mocked.

'And you know how to get it, I suppose,' Danny said.

'I know giving these plans away is madness, when the Russians will pay handsomely for them.' Boots sniffed. 'So, what've those Germans promised you? A revolution? Arms and explosives? You and your mates will become top dogs? Line all those royals, those industrialists and politicians, those rich up against a wall and shoot them? Just you remember, boy, I intend to be one of those rich. And I don't think I'd like the idea of being shot. In fact, I'd rather like the idea of doing some of the shooting.' He waved the pistol and smirked. 'He's a traitor, Mary. Your loving brother's a bomber and a thief—'

'Shut up! He isn't,' Mary barked.

Boots laughed. 'And a fool. There will always be the rich and the poor, and people like him at the bottom of the pile thinking they can change it all. He thinks them blowing up houses and shooting a few people will make a difference. He can believe that if he wants. His lot can have the glory, but me, I'll take the cash.'

'How long do you think you'll stay alive when my friends find out?' Danny said.

'Long enough if you think that fat man's going to

come and help you. Blackmailing you, is that what he's doing? Figures. He's got money, so it's the power he wants, son. Trust me, he's playing you good and proper. He might be protecting you for the moment, but it's only until he gets what he wants, and then he'll cut you lose.'

'You don't know anything,' Danny said.

'I know I'm going to take great pleasure in killing her.' He scowled at Mary. 'This is a big empty house. You three are going to vanish inside it. Maybe I'll give you a room each. You can have your old one in the attic, if you want, Mary. As for me, I'm going to take a nice evening stroll to Marble Arch to meet a man carrying a wad of cash, and then take a nice boat trip to America. By the time they find you lot, I'll be long gone.'

Boots lifted the gun higher and pointed it towards Daniel Finch.

'You first, Mr Anarchist.'

25

FEAR IN THE DARK

'GET HIM!' came a shout from behind Boots.

Several ill-dressed children charged across the drawing room. The Butler's head slewed around in panic. Danny dropped to the ground, pulling Mary beside him, just as there was a bright flash and a terrific bang. The bullet crashed into the wall. Almost immediately, Boots spun around and fired twice more into the drawing room. There came a tinkling of glass and screams of *'He's got a gun'* and *'Hide!'*

The next moment, Boots was off. He dashed away through the drawing room, past the startled faces of the Irregulars.

The echo of the blast was ringing in Mary's ears when she heard Danny shout, 'We've got to stop him.' Quickly up, she flew through the drawing room and spied the frightened Irregulars peeping out from behind settees and chairs and from under tables. Her brother was already ahead of her. Daniel slipped through the open window and, as she reached it, another shot rang out. The bullet crashed into the wooden frame. The glass pane shattered, showering splinters across Mary.

'Midge!' Danny cried.

'He missed by a mile,' she shouted back.

Boots made the gate and dashed across the road with Danny following. Heedless to the danger, Mary was not far behind. Wiggins, the Irregulars and Archie, further back, chased after them.

Ahead of her was the long stretch of a deserted street. The lampposts rose as islands in pools of light with great swathes of darkness between, the trees trembling their shadows on the pavement. Mary could just make out Boots and Danny and the clatter of their echoing foot-steps ahead.

'He's going to the Russians! To Marble Arch!' Danny bellowed.

'I'm coming,' Mary shouted back.

Boots turned. He levelled the gun and there came two bright flashes and two sharp bangs. Mary saw Danny dodge away and roll across the ground, and heard a scream. For a second, she thought he had been shot. To her relief, Danny picked himself up and kept up the chase.

'That's six,' she mumbled softly. 'He'll have to reload, and he ain't doing that while running.'

Mary bent her head and doggedly followed, passing a dark-suited man lying on the ground. He was moaning and clutching his bloody thigh. Another man, similarly dressed, was tending him. She recognised them as the ones who raided the warehouse—Major Carshaw's men were here as well.

Someone grabbed her arm and she was spun around. The lady with the severe face, the one sketching in the park, had hold of her.

'Leave this to us and stop getting in the way,' she growled.

Without a thought, Mary struck out. The lady screamed and tumbled onto the ground. She was running again. Ahead of her, Danny caught up with Boots. The Butler swung the gun, catching Danny who fell back into the darkness.

The clatter of footsteps came from all around now. In a wild panic, Boots swung his pistol in a wide arc, squeezing the trigger. The hammer clicked dully against the spent cartridge cases. He looked around, desperate for an escape. Boots ran into the middle of the road, crouched and pulled frantically at a manhole cover. It came free with a mighty heave and he fell backwards with the effort. He kicked the portfolio into the opening ready to follow it.

As he scrambled upright, Mary caught him off balance. She pushed him with her feet and he tumbled away. Swiftly, before he had time to recover, Mary climbed down the ladder. Her only thought was to retrieve the plans. She was aware that several men were rushing towards the Butler and her brother, but the plans were more important at that moment. With them, even if Daniel was arrested, she would have the leverage she needed.

The bottom of the hole was dark. A weak light shone from another tunnel in front of her. She quickly realised she was in a small passageway, an access way leading to a larger space. In the spill of the light, she could just make out the black portfolio as a darker shadow on the ground. She grasped it. The clanging of footsteps on the ladder came from behind and above her. A quick glance back and she realised that it was Boots scurrying down, chasing after her and the plans.

Her first thought was that she had entered a sewer. But as she exited the access passage, she knew exactly where she was: in the underground railway tunnel leading towards Baker Street. She was standing on a bed of sharp loose black stones and gravel. In the distance she could see the mouth of the tunnel. The dim light that shone there, from the station platforms she could see in the distance, barely illuminated the passage she was in. Two sets of metal rails resting on wooden sleepers extended in front and behind her, also fading into the blackness of the tunnel. The brick walls were blackened with soot, slimy ooze trickling down in places. Even the sleepers were black, while the rails shone brightly. The sulphurous smell of burnt coal hung thickly in the air. Above her was a high-arched roof.

'Give me that back, Finch,' she heard Boots scream. The echo of his voice bounced wildly off the walls and receded, fading into the gloom.

Mary stumbled and ran towards the platforms ahead of her. In her panic, she tripped and fell, her knee crunching against the sharp stones. She cried out in pain. Gingerly, she got back on her feet and limped away from the voice behind her.

She felt the rails tremble and heard a low buzzing noise. A train was coming. She glanced fearfully over her shoulders, but could not see it. The sound it made, though, was getting louder. She could hear the rhythmic clacking of wheels crossing points and their screech against the steel rails. Suddenly, she could make out a light moving against the curve of the tunnel walls, stretching the shadows and filling the space with brightness that was growing with each passing second.

Mary fought back her panic. Her heart pounded, as loud as the approaching train. The roar of the engine echoed off the dark walls and seemed to be everywhere at once. She worried the onrushing train would carry her away. Every twenty feet or so was a brick buttress. It was all she could do to squeeze tightly behind one.

With a clattering rush, the train was upon her. The cold white light on the front sped past. She gasped a deep breath, clutched her ears and closed her eyes tightly. The engine roared and drowned her screams of terror. Hot, acrid smoke and fiery steam from the boiler engulfed her. The train hurtled by, rows and rows of carriages flashing dizzily along in a thunderous clanging, jangling rattle that shook the ground and echoed all around her.

When it passed, sulphurous smoke hung like a foul smelly fog. Mary gasped for breath. The train sped away, the bright red light on the back of the rear carriage grew smaller and smaller, the clattering noise fading in the distance.

Mary clutched the walls with trembling hands. Even though her legs wobbled, she was moving again, more out of fear that another train might appear than anything else. In the dim light, she hurried along, constantly stumbling and tripping on the uneven rock-strewn ground.

Then she remembered Boots. She could hear him shouting her name. He was somewhere nearby. Mary ran in panic, clutching the portfolio, hoping that Danny had escaped from Major Carshaw's men and was safe.

26

BAKER STREET
UNDERGROUND STATION

THE TUNNEL ISSUED out into the magnificent Baker Street station, with its wonderful arched roof. The platforms on either side of the rails were empty of people. It was late, and soon the station would close for the night.

Mary scrambled up from the tracks. She was dirty and dusty; the stench of smoke was in her nose. Her knee was bleeding from her tumble. Still, she clutched her prize in triumph.

She looked for the way out. The exit was at the other end of the platform. There was no time to lose.

'Mary,' Boots shouted from the darkness not far behind her. She skidded and stopped. The exit was too far away; he would see her if she tried to go there, she'd be an easy target. In a wild panic, she threw herself back down on to the tracks. The platform slightly overhung the rails, enough for her to curl and squeeze into the dark shadowy space.

'All right, I was wrong, I admit it,' shouted Boots, his voice nearer. 'I overreacted. Let's talk about this.'

Mary heard Boots grunting with the effort of climbing up from the tracks to the platform. She could hear his footsteps on the stone floor. She held her breath for fear of making a sound and followed his steps until she realised he was standing just above her. She pressed further back, fearing he knew where she was hiding.

'Come on, Mary.' He was panting hard. 'So, we've had our differences. There's no denying that. But we can work this out to our mutual convenience.'

His shadow was falling across the ground beside her.

'I know you don't trust me. I get that. But I'm a businessman. The money is more important to me than anything else. I was just angry before when I said those things back then. I reacted badly. But why spoil a good thing, Mary? Let's forget the past. We can let bygones be bygones, can't we? Come on, what say you?'

Mary pressed harder against the wall; she pulled her legs in tight and forced herself to stop trembling. She didn't trust him. Twice he'd tried to kill her. If she made a sound, if she showed herself, he'd be on her in a heartbeat.

But there was desperation in his voice. Behind him, Mary understood, either Danny or the Major's men must be following. If they were, she would be in danger of losing her prize to them, rather than Boots.

She heard a click. There was a tinkling sound like pennies dropping on to the ground. Something flashed past her eyes and clinked on to the stones in front of her. It bounced up to balance on one of the rails. She saw the dull gleam of a brass cartridge case. Boots had emptied his revolver of the spent shell casings. She heard the snick as each new round was pushed into a chamber. Mary cursed silently. In her panic to get away from Boots, she had forgotten… his gun was empty.

'Look, Mary,' he shouted, 'it's like this. Your brother is in trouble. You're right—you're a clever girl: those plans will help him. But only if I'm there to negotiate the deal. That's because I know these things. We're talking about blackmailing Mr Holmes and you know I have practice in that business.'

He stepped away and Mary heard his feet shuffle along the platform.

'We can make this work for both of us, Mary. I just need those plans for a couple of hours. I have a friend. He can photograph them. Don't you see, Mary? I can have the pictures and you'll still have the real things to trade with. Mr Holmes won't know about the photographs, he won't suspect a thing. He'll be so anxious to save himself that he'll be willing to forget all about your brother. He may even lose the records he has on him just to get the plans back.'

Boots paused. Mary screwed herself even more tightly inside her hiding space. She wiped the sweat from her eyes.

'Imagine that, Mary. Danny will be as free as a bird. Come on, what say you? Is it a deal or what? There'll be a good amount of cash as well. You and Danny can have enough to become independent.'

His voice was coming from somewhere along the platform. If she kept quiet, he might assume she left the station. But Boots was still talking.

'Take Danny away, Mary. Take him somewhere safe, where no one knows what he did to the Fullers. Be a family again. That's what you really want, isn't it?'

Mary ground her teeth. The Fullers were alive. She said it over and over again in her mind.

'It's a good deal, Mary. Everyone gets what they want.'

No, no, no, she said to herself. *He's lying.* She was grim. If she showed herself, he would get what he wanted, and she a bullet. She crouched lower.

A movement caught her eye. The empty cartridge case resting on the rail trembled. She watched it vibrate and slip off with a slight bounce. She slowly turned her head and looked down the mouth of the tunnel she only recently exited. Several dirty grey rats bolted across the sleepers towards her. She flinched as one scrambled over her toes. Her heart pounded increasingly loud and fast.

A train was coming.

If she stayed where she was, she'd be between the platform and the wheels of the train. How low were the carriages? How wide was the train? She couldn't risk staying where she was. But if she could cross the tracks just as the train came in, it would be between her and Boots. He might never see her.

To her horror, she realised another train was approaching from the opposite direction. Both would arrive at the station almost together. Now she could not rush across the tracks.

Come on, Mr Boots. She willed him to leave.

She could hear the clacking of the wheels getting louder.

Now she could see the lights from the tunnels becoming brighter. The air was rushing past her, pushed forward by the engine. The tracks were vibrating. The small stones were shaking and clacking against the metal rails.

'What say you, Mary? We have a deal, don't we?' Mr Boots pleaded.

The roar of the engines was filling her ears. The headlights shone blindingly. She ached to move.

Wait, wait, wait, Mary told herself.

Her heart pounded.

Wait. Wait.

The sweat ran down her face.

Wait.

The train loomed nearer.

In one swift motion, she scrambled over the lip of the platform, throwing the portfolio ahead of her. A second later, both trains thundered in. The one on her side caught the hem of her dress and spun her around as the material tore. She saw the look of horror on the driver's face. The next moment, she tumbled across the stone floor and away from the leather case with the plans.

She scrambled to grasp the portfolio just as Boots swivelled around. Through the corner of her eye, she saw him raise the gun. She barely heard the bang above the rattling noise of the engine. The bullet smashed into one of the ceramic tiles that lined the wall.

Mary ran. Clutching her prize, she dashed headlong through a tunnel, his clattering steps just behind her. She made for a flight of stairs that several people were coming down. As she clawed her way through them, Boots grabbed her dress. She tumbled backwards. At the same moment, Mary felt the muzzle of the gun swipe across her face. There was a stinging pain and she crashed to the bottom of the stairs.

Before she knew it, he snatched the leather case and dashed up the stairs. Those coming down the steps, taken completely by surprise, could only look at him as he charged past them.

'Miss, you all right?' An elderly man was helping her stand. He held out a handkerchief towards her.

'W-wh-where is he?' Mary stuttered. A wave of nausea addled her brain as she struggled to rise. The pain from the blow throbbed. She was aware of the crowd closing around her.

'Someone get the coppers,' a lady shouted.

'A robbery—and with a gun,' a woman cried out.

'On the Underground, of all places!' another complained.

'Where is he?' Mary shouted over them. To everyone's amazement, she launched herself towards the stairs. Ignoring the pain, she scrambled up them, almost tripping in her haste. She left behind her gasps and shouts for her to wait for aid. But there was no time to lose. If she was to help her brother, she had to catch Boots, and she knew where he was going.

27

SPEAKERS' CORNER

MARY DID NOT EXPLAIN herself to the ticket collector at the entrance. She flew past him, ignoring his shouts for her to stop and didn't she know it was against the law to travel without a ticket? She ran down Marylebone Road. After several attempts, she finally managed to hail a hansom.

'Mister, get me to Marble Arch in a hurry,' Mary shouted, 'and I'll give you five bob.'

'Is this a joke?' The cabbie peered down at her. He could not help but notice her sooty, dirty face and dress, her dishevelled appearance and the dribble of blood from the cut on her head. She looked like an urchin, if anything.

Mary fumbled in her purse and took out several coins.

'Here! Five shillings.' She handed it up to him.

The cabbie scrutinised the coins, his eyes widening.

'Get in!' he shouted. Mary slumped wearily into the seat and heard him say, 'Marble Arch in a hurry, is it?' He snapped his whip and his horse stumbled away, sending her tumbling further back inside the cab. 'Hold on to your hat, miss.'

What began as a trot soon became a fast canter. They bumped along, weaving in and out of the slower traffic; every so often, the whip cracked and on they went. The driver dashed through junctions, narrowly missing other cabs. She could hear him barking orders to pedestrians to get out of the way.

Mary gripped the seat tightly as she got her breath back. She felt sick, annoyed that she hadn't been brave enough to make a rush to the exit at Baker Street. Boots's gun was empty. She ground her teeth in rage because she knew it was. But she hadn't been able to think straight when she heard his voice, and all she'd done was give him time to reload. Her hesitation rankled—it cost her dearly. She dabbed the blood away from the throbbing cut on her head, and seethed in anger.

And this excursion was no more than a long shot. Boots said he was going to take a nice stroll to Marble Arch. She could still hear Danny's voice shouting that the Butler was going to meet the Russians; she hoped she was right. She could not give up her last chance to help her brother. She gambled on being right.

After a hectic ride, they arrived at the corner of Hyde Park.

'Was that quick enough, miss?' the cabbie asked. Then he looked up and joked, 'I see the dreamers are about. They'd make a stuffed bird laugh!'

Speakers' Corner, as it was called, was still crowded, even at that late an hour. Several groups of shadowy grey-black men were huddled together, listening to and heckling a woman standing on a box. Behind her were more ladies and a banner that proudly proclaimed, *'Lips that touch alcohol shall not touch ours.'* Not far from them was another group with a banner, *'Capitalism is the Devil's Creed.'* The groups were competing and both speakers were determined to outdo the other.

Mary ambled over and glanced around her. Her curiosity brought her here once, many years ago, and afterwards, Grandpa Dibble told her its history.

Just over a hundred years ago, this was a place of execution—Tyburn gallows stood nearby. The grim irony was not lost on her: this was the place where they'd hanged murderers and traitors. But before being hanged, the condemned was allowed to address the crowd. The executions drew large numbers of people and became an event, like some macabre play where tickets could be purchased for spots that gave the most advantageous views.

She pressed her way amongst the crowd, oblivious to the speakers. She was desperately looking for the one face she would recognise. There were so many, so close together, she struggled to see them properly in the dark.

Before long, she realised that her best bet would be to stand away so she could take a wider view. And she did not want to be standing in front of Boots, to be near and unprepared. But look as she did, carefully scrutinising the faces and the build and the gait of the men, she could not see the Butler.

She prayed and hoped that she was right, that he was here. When she found him, somehow she must confront him. She felt safe in the open. Boots would not be foolish enough to brandish his pistol amongst the crowd that was here. Even so, she missed Archie. She would feel safer if he were with her.

She wended her way around. Still, she could not see Boots. Soon she was perspiring, hot with the worry that she made a mistake. The cold fingers of doubt gripped her. She feared her gamble was a bust. If Boots's business was to meet some Russian gentleman, perhaps he had done so already and was gone. Perhaps she'd misheard his words or mistaken their meaning. Perhaps his intention was to meet the Russians at another time. Her thoughts were straying, drifting away into uncertainty. She had failed her brother.

'Think, Mary Finch, think,' she mumbled. 'What would Mr Holmes do?' She gritted her teeth and refocused her mind. Her head throbbed and pulsated. She grunted—no, it made sense. Boots had an appointment. He'd indicated it was at Marble Arch. He'd given the impression that it would take place soon. Danny said it was the Russians the Butler was courting. It was reasonable to believe he was here.

Then she realised her mistake. She was looking at the crowd. He would not be amongst them. He'd be near, but away from them. No doubt he'd chosen this place because it was a public space. She was certain again. He would be nearby.

Before long, she walked a complete circle around Speakers' Corner. Behind the crowds, the park was gloomy and vanished into the darkness, while the houses fronting it were ablaze with light. Traffic moved smoothly along the roads. People listened to the speakers. She neither heard nor saw them; her attention was elsewhere. Her eyes fell on the splendid four-wheeled carriage drawn up on Bayswater Road. The carriage's door had a coat of arms she did not recognise, but it spoke of power and tradition.

A man in uniform, gold braids and polished brass buttons; a neat red stripe down the legs of his black trousers; a peaked cap set importantly on his head, was standing beside it. He looked like an officer of some rank. When she noticed him flick a cigarette away to join several others on the ground, her heart fluttered. She was right after all. He was waiting and had been there a while.

Now that her eyes were accustomed to the gloom, she noticed other things. Across the road, almost hidden in the shadows, someone else waited. At first, Mary thought it was Boots. But the watcher remained hidden while gazing at the carriage. He was wearing a bowler hat, the meaning of which Mary now understood. Under the trees of Hyde Park that bordered the road, another similarly attired man waited. And a third, further back.

Near the crowd beside one of the speakers was the young lady from Regent's Park, she with the severe face and the sketchpad. Her gaze, though, like the men's, was fixed on the carriage. Despite her injured face, she too was waiting.

Mary glanced around. Where was Major Carshaw? If his men were here, surely, he too would be nearby.

The uniformed man spoke to someone inside the carriage and a cigarette was passed to him. He struck a match against the wheel and, as he brought the cigarette up, his eyes rose to stare along the road. He dropped both match and cigarette to the ground and crushed them under his shoes.

Boots was coming steadily along the road. His head was down and his collar was pulled up as if he wanted to conceal his face. Even though he was a distance away, it was definitely him. In one hand, he was carrying the large leather portfolio, folded in half. His other hand was deep inside his pocket. No doubt, she supposed, it was clutching his gun. And no doubt, the carriage he was walking towards belonged to the Russians with whom he was about to do business.

It troubled her that the men and women in the shadows did nothing while Boots sauntered along, clutching state secrets under his arm. They must have seen him, but still they remained where they were, hidden and watchful.

Another elegant carriage was arriving. Mary saw it. This one drew up on Park Lane and stopped beside the open lawns across the road from the houses in front of Speakers' Corner. She recognised the coat of arms displayed on the side: a black eagle with wings outspread held a shield on which was another black eagle. It was the same one she had seen at Barnes some days ago. It was the same emblem worn by the sailors of the *Prinz Wilhelm*, anchored in the channel at Gravesend.

The German Ambassador had arrived.

28

SHOTS IN THE DARK

MARY CREPT CAREFULLY TOWARDS BOOTS. She kept to the shadows, fearful that he would see her. She had to intercept him before he reached the Russian officer and his carriage. But her mind flew back to what happened at Baker Street. She had not been brave enough then.

The thought that if she had been, she would still have the plans focused her mind. Dwelling on what could have been was a useless exercise. The here and now was what she needed to concentrate on. Even so, her idea was a mad one. It smacked of sheer desperation. But the cold realisation that it was all she could do made her strong.

It was simple, she told herself: get near enough to Boots to snatch the portfolio, and then run. He would not be expecting her, surprise was on her side. She would have to dodge not only Boots, but also Major Carshaw's people. Would the Russian Officer get involved? Would

Boots draw his pistol? She was grateful it was night. With luck, she would escape into the darkness of the park.

She readied herself. As Boots came nearer, Major Carshaw's people slipped out from where they were hiding. They either had not noticed or were not interested in her. She crept closer.

The Butler stopped and hesitated. He looked around anxiously. Carshaw's people did not come nearer. Satisfied, Boots moved quickly towards the carriage.

The Russian Officer's hand flicked the flap of his holster open and gripped the butt of his pistol. He'd spotted the Major's people. But almost immediately, a hand came out from the carriage and rested on his shoulder. Slowly, he released his grip on his pistol and closed the flap of the holster, and waited.

No one was paying Mary any attention; everyone's focus was on Boots. This was her chance. She wouldn't get another. Her heart thumped wildly in her chest. Her mouth was dry. She felt her legs move, carrying her forward instinctively.

Suddenly, a dark figure rushed out from the bushes ahead of her. It sprinted across the pavement, and a moment later collided with Boots. The force of the impact flung the Butler to the ground. With a skilful dip of a hand, the figure grasped the leather portfolio, turned and ran towards the crowds on Speakers' Corner.

Daniel Finch sprinted away. Just as he made the

crowds, Mary heard a terrible scream, and then three quick loud bangs. Then a fourth. Then a fifth. She glimpsed his arm held high in the air, his hand clutching a revolver. He'd discharged five shots into the air.

The crowd broke into a shrieking panic. People scattered, running here and there to get away from the madman with a gun. They ran headlong into Major Carshaw's people, completely overwhelming them as they tried to give chase.

Mary followed the fleeing figure as he wove his way through the crowd. She knew where he was going and rushed in a diagonal direction to intercept him before he reached the carriage of the German Ambassador. She was several paces behind as she cleared the crowd.

'Danny!' she shouted. 'Wait, Danny!'

Her brother swung around at the call of his name. He was panting hard from the excitement. His face was slick with sweat. He scowled at her.

'Damn it, Midge. Get away from me,' he snapped.

'No, I won't,' she shouted, rushing up and grasping his arms. 'I can help you fight Mr Holmes. Danny, the Fullers are alive. Don't you see? Mr Holmes hasn't got a thing on you if they're alive.'

Danny tried to pull away, but Mary clung on. He glanced over his shoulders. The driver of the German carriage was shouting, '*Herr Fuller, Komm bitte her. Jetzt bitte.*' He beckoned Danny energetically.

'Midge, stop interfering.' There was anguish in

Danny's voice. He was pleading. 'There's too much at stake. I know what I'm doing.'

'You can't give them the plans, Danny. I won't let you. We can fight Mr Holmes. I know you didn't kill anyone. I know you ain't no anarchist. Please, Danny,' she implored, shaking him.

'*Herr Fuller*,' the driver shouted urgently, pointing to the panicking crowd and some policemen who were arriving on the scene. '*Schnell, Herr Fuller, schnell. Geben sie mir die pläne. Schnell.*'

Mary reached out and grabbed at the portfolio. As she tugged it, Danny pulled it back and yanked her forward until they came together. His face was against hers.

'You don't understand, Midge. I ain't no traitor. Nor's Mr Holmes,' he whispered harshly. 'What I'm doing has to be done for the good of everyone. Now get away and leave me alone.'

Suddenly, he pushed Mary hard and sent her sprawling across the ground. To her horror, he levelled the gun at her. There was a wild look in his eyes as he squeezed the trigger. The gun barked and Mary fell backwards as she tried to scramble away. When she looked again, she saw him throw the portfolio into the Ambassador's carriage. Then, Daniel Finch rushed away into the night.

Mary sat on her haunches and screamed in anguish. She could not believe it. Danny shot at her. She glanced down and urgently patted her stomach and chest, searching for the wound, but she was untouched. He missed. The understanding that he was capable of such an awful deed struck her like a blow. Daniel Finch, her brother, not only betrayed his country, he was not only an anarchist, a bomber, a thief, a turncoat, but he'd tried to murder her.

She made to rise and follow him, but her legs refused to work. It felt as if the life had been drained from them and she slumped into herself and slipped to the ground. Her mind went completely blank.

When she looked up, Major Carshaw was standing beside her. He was calmly leaning on his umbrella as he held out a hand for her to take. Mary glared at him. He shook his head slowly as if he was dealing with a wilful child, withdrew his hand and stood upright. She followed his gaze. He was watching the carriage of the German Ambassador slowly make its way through the busy traffic on Park Lane. There was a strange look on the Major's face; a look she could not understand.

'Why don't you arrest him?' Mary cried. 'You're bleedin' torpedo plans are in his carriage.'

'And start a diplomatic incident, Miss Finch?' the Major said matter-of-factly.

'I don't understand,' Mary said, her head falling low. 'You could have stopped him. You had all your people in position. Why didn't you stop him?'

'Stop whom, Miss Finch? Mr Boots? The German Ambassador? Your brother? And what is there not to understand? Your brother is a traitor. He's passed on some valuable information to a foreign power. We'll arrest him, try him and hang him. He even tried to kill you. It is lucky for you that he missed his shot. Very lucky, it appears. Your head is bleeding.' Carshaw fiddled with his moustache and shook his head again. 'Unfortunately, Mr Boots, like your brother, has flown.'

Mary looked at the ground. She fought back her tears for as long as she could, then felt them wet her cheeks.

She heard the Major sigh. 'Why do you not go home, Miss Finch?' he said. 'You have caused us enough trouble these past few days. Finally, things will be allowed to run their course. You have a cut on your head that needs tending. Shall I call you a cab?'

Mary was silent. He shook his head a third time and walked away. She gazed forlornly at the ground and wept. All her hopes, to be reunited with her brother; to be a family once more; to hear what he remembered of their parents, of what it was like when she was young, had vanished in the instance of a gunshot. Once more, she was alone.

Seated on the ground, she cried long and hard.

❋ 29 ❋

A WARRANT FOR A MURDERER

MARY TRUDGED BACK to Baker Street. She felt lost. She could have walked and walked and walked, and if she never arrived, it would be of no consequence whatsoever —no one would miss her; no one would care, especially not a brother who tried to kill her. A sickness twisted her stomach and a lump swelled in her throat that she could not be rid of. She revelled in the ache of her head that said how stupid she was; how remarkably unclever she was. A dullard if ever there was one. His shot must have missed by just a fraction.

By the time she reached the Dibbles' pie shop, her tears had dried, but the taste of salt was still on her lips. It was well past midnight. She slumped against the door and cried again until she could cry no more. The few people who passed her that night must have thought her homeless, some tramp resting in a doorway. But she did not care.

When she looked up, she noticed her shadow was gone. He was no longer needed, she knew. It was all over, all done with. Her hopes of saving her brother, of being a family once more, vanished.

The minutes ticked into hours as she sat in silent contemplation. How could he do this? Sell secrets to the enemy? He tricked her. Mr Boots was right. Her red eyes rose up to the dark windows of 221B. The great Detective was either asleep or out. Did he know his brother was the same as hers? Both were traitors?

The clock struck two, then three, and then four. A thought kept on returning to her mind. Sherlock Holmes once said, *'There is nothing more deceptive than an obvious fact.'* Why it should haunt her now, she did not know, yet there it was, mingling freely with another: just how strangely the good Major acted.

The clock struck five. The skies lightened. She shivered in the cool air and saw the dew dampen the pavements. Dawn was fast approaching. By six strikes, the day was bright, and by the half, Baker Street was getting busy.

What did the Major mean, *'Things will be allowed to run their course'*? He'd seemed almost pleased. It was as if some burden had been lifted when he said that. She'd seen it in his eyes, she was sure she had.

The door behind her opened and she almost fell back. Archie, dressed to go out, stood above her.

'You've been sitting here all night?' he asked and Mary nodded. 'We looked last night,' he said, 'but when we couldn't find you, we thought we'd make an early start and look again.' He exhaled with relief. 'Hungry?' he asked and she nodded again.

He brushed her hair away and looked at the cut, a scab forming and the angry bruise around it; he looked at her swollen red eyes, but said nothing. He helped her to rise.

'Grandma, breakfast for Mary,' he shouted. 'Bacon, eggs, fried bread, the lot. Looks like she could use a feed.'

Over breakfast, Mary told Archie all that happened. She did not tell him how Daniel tried to kill her, though. She could not bear to tell him that. The hurt ran far too deep. She was still angry that she'd allowed Boots to take back the plans from her at Baker Street. Had she managed to hold on to them, then none of this would have happened. But even as she said that, she knew it was not true. Fate conspired against her; it'd moved the pieces in a game to which she did not know the rules. Somehow, things would have ended up the same.

As she climbed into bed in the small storeroom, exhausted by the night's events, Archie knocked on the door. He came in with a solemn face and handed her the morning newspaper.

Mary groaned.

At the bottom of the front page, a grainy photograph of her brother stared back at her.

MURDERER SOUGHT!

A Warrant has been issued for the Apprehension of Daniel Fuller in connection to the bombings of several properties in London, including the attempted murder of Mr Fairchild Rentham, 56, a wealthy Industrialist, and the slaying of Mr and Mrs Fuller of Gravesend, Kent, along with affiliations to the International Solidarity Revolutionary Movement.

The suspect, last seen near Hyde Park yesterday evening, is described as: Aged 18, Height 5 feet 9 inches. Complexion fair, light brown hair, no Whiskers or Moustache, but not shaved for several days, Lean Build; Dress, dark ill-fitting clothes.

TWO HUNDRED POUNDS REWARD will be paid by Her Majesty's Government to any person who shall give such Information and Evidence as shall lead to the discovery of the Murderer, and the Secretary of State for the Home Department will advise the grant of HER Majesty's MOST GRACIOUS PARDON to any accomplice, not being the person who actually committed the Murder, who shall give such Evidence as shall lead to a like result.

. . .

WHEN ARCHIE LEFT, MARY LAY BACK AND STARED AT the ceiling. So, Mr Holmes made up his mind, and any deal he had with Daniel Finch, he reneged on. She was loath to admit it, but Boots was right: Mr Holmes had been using Danny. She could shed no more tears, and so her mind began to trawl through the events that led her to be here, reading this article. So many things did not make sense, yet at the same time, paradoxically, they did. And that she could not explain.

The Fullers were alive, she knew that, and yet the Graingers upped sticks and vanished. Was it because the secret was out and they had been working with Mr Holmes all along? Was that why the police reports had been changed, to make a more convincing case against Danny when Mycroft Holmes was ready to cut him loose? She screwed up the paper and flung it on to the floor in anger. The police would be hunting him now.

'Poor *Sergeant* O'Connor,' she seethed. What a mess she made of everything. She ruined his promotion, believing that her brother was no anarchist. Yet, even so, she was sure he wasn't one; otherwise, why draw such attention to stealing secrets from Rentham in such a manner, knowing the hue and cry it would cause? Surely no one would want that? What was it Daniel said? He could open a combination lock safe with his eyes closed, and wasn't Rentham's safe a combination lock?

Daniel was no more than a pawn in Mr Holmes's game. The French, the Italians, the Russians—each would pay handsomely for the plans. And the money, if Danny were an anarchist, would fund the cause for years to come. Yet he'd said the plans had to be given away, to the Germans and no one else. Perhaps there was more to be gained from the Germans for an ambitious man like Mycroft Holmes.

How could such a seemingly solid citizen be a traitor? She'd thought the notion fanciful, once—absurd, even. And her brother insisted he was no traitor, nor was Mr Holmes. He'd said she was getting in the way. Then he'd tried to kill her. She saw the muzzle of the revolver. She shivered as she recollected the terrible bang and blinked as she saw the flash. He was barely two feet away. Even now, as she lay in bed, the smell of gunpowder was in her nose. The front of her dress was peppered with small burns. What he was doing was for everyone's good, he'd said, but, isn't that what an anarchist would say?

She closed her eyes as the questions flew and threaded their way into her mind. 'No,' she murmured. In her bones, she felt as if there was something else going on.

Finally worn out, Mary slept fitfully.

IT WAS EARLY EVENING WHEN SHE AWOKE WITH A START.

After the Grimwig affair, when she was ill, Dr Watson gave Grandpa Dibble a copy of one of his books to read to her. She found the book and sat on the bed.

Dr Watson said to Sherlock Holmes, she read, *'I'm afraid that the facts are so obvious that you will find little credit to be gained out of the case.'*

And Homes replied, *'There is nothing more deceptive than an obvious fact. Besides, we may chance to hit upon some other obvious facts which may have been by no means obvious to Mr Lestrade.'*

She dressed quickly.

'Archie,' Mary shouted and rushed to find him, 'where's the Diogenes Club?'

30

THE DIOGENES CLUB

THEY STOPPED several hansoms until they found a cabbie who knew the whereabouts of the club. The driver said he remembered taking several *odd* gentlemen there on occasions. He shook his head at Mary.

'It's a gentlemen's club, miss, you ain't getting in,' he said, looked at Archie, smiled smugly and winked. 'You ain't either, son!'

He dropped them at the St James's end of Pall Mall. It had just gone six. And even though it was Saturday, she expected Mycroft Holmes would be there. Routine was important to him; she remembered his comment about his habits. He ran on rails, she recalled.

She saw Mycroft Holmes immediately as she entered the hall. He was seated in a large luxurious room behind a glass-panelled door, perusing a newspaper. What looked like a glass of brandy was by his side. Opposite and away from him sat Major Carshaw, smoking a cigar and reading a book. Both men, rapt in what they were doing, seemed oblivious of each other. Around them were individuals doing the same or similar. Strangely, each sat in an alcove or a corner, or behind something; none were seated next to another. It was if none knew the others. That, or they were keeping deliberately apart.

'Mister,' she said to the attendant, 'please may I speak to Mr Holmes?'

The man looked her up and down, his face contorted. At first, Mary assumed it was because of how she was dressed, still in the same soot-blackened clothes from yesterday, the bruise now prominent on her forehead.

'Speak?' the man said, alarmed. 'Do you know where you are, miss?' He placed a finger against his lips and shushed her.

'He's just there.' Mary pointed.

'He can't be disturbed,' the man whispered. Gripping her arm, he began to lead her back to the exit.

'But mister, it's important.'

'So is what he's doing.'

'Reading the newspaper?' Archie said. The man shushed him and grasped his arm as well.

Mary looked over her shoulders as she was led away.

'You must be quiet,' the attendant said and hushed her. Yet again, he pulled her along. With a twist, Mary freed herself and, to the man's absolute horror, charged towards the room in which Mycroft Holmes sat. Even as she barged open the door, she was aware of everyone's eyes swivelling to see who had entered in such a distasteful manner. And when they saw it was a girl, she heard audible gasps of disbelief, quickly followed by absolute silence.

'Miss, miss,' the attendant shouted, 'this is unheard of. You can't do this. This is a gentleman's club. Miss, what do you think—'

He stopped suddenly, all eyes were now looking at him. His hand shot up to his mouth. Flushing scarlet, he reached out to grab Mary's arm, but Mary was determined. She stepped sideways and stood in front of Mycroft Holmes.

'You and your games. Who do you think you are? Well? Just who?' she shouted.

Mycroft Holmes gazed at her in annoyance and carefully folder the newspaper, clasped it and arose. He glared at the man employed to keep people out.

'Well?' Mary shouted. 'What've you got to say for yourself?' He did not reply. 'Nothing, eh? Is that it?' Mary continued, unabashed. Even though he now towered above her, her blood was up and she wasn't about to back down. 'Too ashamed, are you?'

'Sir,' the attendant apologised and clamped his mouth shut again.

Mycroft Holmes's eyes shifted back to her. She saw the anger burning in his gaze suddenly vanish, and his eyes took on a peculiar light, a faraway meditative look.

To her astonishment, he smiled and gently took her by the arm. With his other hand, he indicated they should go to another room.

'Ah!' the attendant said. 'Yes, sir. Of course, sir. The Strangers' Room, sir. This way, madam, I mean miss… I mean…' and again he fell quiet, his face continuing to burn red as he scanned the room and the many eyes looking at him accusingly.

Mr Holmes beckoned Major Carshaw to follow. It was all so strange that Mary had to glance back. No one said a word. No one was whispering or appeared curious as to what just happened. Whatever indignation creased their faces earlier was no longer there. In fact, whatever they were doing before she entered the room, they were doing again, as if nothing had happened. The only sound she heard was the gentle rustling of newspaper pages being turned. She saw what the cabbie meant when he called them *odd*.

The Strangers' Room was an elegant space, sparsely furnished and seemingly seldom used. Mary was escorted to a set of chairs and invited to sit in one. Mycroft Holmes sat opposite her. Major Carshaw sat beside them, while Archie remain standing.

'There are rules, young lady,' Mr Holmes said softly. 'I will not bore you with them, other than to say that they define us. I will not state the obvious other than that.'

'I don't give a fig for your rules,' Mary said pugnaciously, perching on the edge of her chair. 'Not where my brother is concerned.'

'I see that clearly,' he said. 'It is also clear that you are upset, and you have been crying. Considerable tears, if we are to judge by the colour of your eyes.'

Mary was about to speak when Mr Holmes indicated that she shouldn't. He spent a minute surveying her in much the same way he did in the pie shop; in fact, in much the same way he'd done a minute ago when she'd thought he was angry. His steady and unyielding gaze made her apprehensive now she calmed a little and had time to think. But she puffed herself up, determined not to show any nerve.

Then Mycroft Holmes sat back and became comfortable. 'Archie,' he said, 'may we have a few minutes alone with Mary? She is perfectly safe.'

Archie hung back, clearly reluctant to leave.

'Go on, Archie.' Mary nodded. 'Wait for me outside. I don't think you're dressed proper for this here place, anyways.'

A heavy silence followed when Archie left. It was only after a minute that Mycroft Holmes spoke.

'Miss Finch is one of those people who pick at loose threads, Major. She picks and picks, and eventually the whole cardigan is unravelled. A way to keep a secret is to tell no one, Miss Finch. And if you cannot do that, then tell a few only. So it is best to take you into our confidence. That way, if and when the cardigan does unravel, we will know who unravelled it, as it will not be us. So, what is it you know, or think you know? But be aware: we will neither confirm nor deny, merely listen.'

'I like a good bedtime story,' the Major said, glancing at his pocket watch. 'We have time, sir.' He sat back, extended his legs and crossed his ankles. Twining his fingers together on his stomach, a glass of brandy between his hands, he waited. The smirk that Mary found so annoying returned to his lips.

31

A GOOD BEDTIME STORY

'THERE ARE a few things I'm unsure of and I'll take a guess at them,' Mary began. 'But firstly, Mr Holmes, I'd like to say that I'm never going to forgive you, even if I live to be a hundred, keeping Danny and me apart like you've done.'

Mycroft Holmes cast an emotionless gaze at her.

'I know you're playing a game, and I know it's a dangerous game, a secret game and a clever game. And I know that Danny is involved. And I know he's involved because of you. I don't know what it is you do, Mr Holmes, but I do know that it's important. And it's no point denying it.

'When I first sees you, you were with Danny. I couldn't understand why you delayed Mr Rentham from going into his office until I realised the big explosion had to coincide with the smaller one that opened the safe. So,

I knew you and Danny was working together. Later, everyone tried to convince me that Danny was an anarchist. But Danny was particular about making sure no one was killed when that bomb went off—he even drew the curtains at the back of the room—and a true anarchist would have loved it if everyone got blown to bits.

'Later, Danny told me he could open a combination lock with his eyes closed. Rentham's safe was a combination lock. So, why blow it open? It was as if someone wanted everyone to know a crime had taken place, as if they wanted the attention. Even though you lot knew Naval plans had been stolen, you convinced Mr Lestrade and Mr Gregson it was personal papers and it was all about blackmail. I didn't understand why you were keeping the coppers in the dark.'

'Naval plans! Whatever gave you that idea?' Major Carshaw looked away as if he was bored.

'You didn't bat an eyelid, Major, when I said your torpedo plans were in the Ambassador's carriage. All you said was you didn't want to have a diplomatic incident. Oh, we both know what was nicked.'

Mycroft Holmes's face wore a silent scold. The Major sipped his drink and looked at her over the rim of the glass.

'Going to Barnes convinced me to go to Gravesend. What a surprise that the Fullers' grave is only a marker as they conveniently disappeared under the Thames. What a surprise to learn that they are alive and living happily in

Wells. Danny didn't kill them after all. But the real surprise was the police reports of the crime that got changed and rearranged overnight after my visit, and the Graingers running away. I know why now.' Mary's eyes flicked to the newspaper Mycroft Holmes still clutched, in particular at the article offering a reward for the apprehension of Daniel Fuller. 'O'Connor was right—two witness statements only on a double murder? That had to change, and quick.

'That was when your people started following me, Major.'

The smile was still on the Major's face, just less so.

'Something else had gone wrong. I only realised what when I saw the bruises on Danny's face. I understand now the visit you made to the pie shop, Mr Holmes. You needed me—and the Irregulars—not to find Danny. He was never missing. You and he were working together, you knew where he was all the time. No, it was to find Mr Boots, because he'd messed up your scheme by taking the plans for himself. You were gambling that I'd be looking for Mr Boots as my only way to find Danny.

'And the Major's been looking out for Danny. You allowed him to escape at that meeting in Limehouse. And it was you who briefed the coppers on the raid on Mr Boots's house in Barnes, and gave Danny time to get away.

'What was clever was how easily I lost my shadow yesterday when I went to Regent's Park. I was always meant to, wasn't I? I was concentrating so much on him, I didn't notice someone else trailing me—the woman with the sketch pad—not until I saw her later. She or her friend was the one who must have told Danny where Boots was, I'm guessing. You used me to find him, but then you forgot about me, didn't you?'

Mycroft Holmes stared back impassively, while the Major shrugged noncommittally.

'I thought Danny was shouting to me about Boots going to see the Russians when we was chasing him.' She shook her head. 'No, Major, it was your people he was shouting to. I realise that now, and I was slow doing so. I guess I was thinking about other things and busy feeling sorry for myself.

'I apologise, Mr Holmes. At first, I thought you was a double agent, and it was the Germans you really worked for. But you're a clever man. The truth struck me only when I woke up this afternoon. All that's happened wasn't to convince *everyone* that Danny was a criminal; it was about convincing the Germans, specifically. And I wondered how the German Ambassador knew to be there last night. All very convenient, wasn't it?'

She was looking at the Major as she said that, who was still spying her over the rim of the brandy glass. Mary turned her gaze back to Mr Holmes.

'You're not the double agent, Mr Holmes—Danny is. Making him out to be a criminal, an anarchist, a thief, a dangerous man on the run, was to make the Germans believe—'

'If you are suggesting your brother is our man, Miss Finch, then why is his picture in each of today's newspapers?' Major Carshaw said casually. 'He is a wanted man —hardly someone we would want working for us. Everyone knows this, and that we will pick him up soon enough.'

'No, you won't, Major,' Mary said. 'The reason his picture is in the papers is to give him some *credibility*. And, anyway, when we first met in the park, how did you know he was my brother? No, Major, this stuff has been a game.'

The major's eyes skewed across to Mycroft Holmes. But Mr Holmes's face was emotionless.

'He shot at you, or are you forgetting?' the Major reminded her. 'And only missed by the grace of God.'

'He was two feet away. He couldn't have possibly missed. Look, my dress is covered in burn marks from the gunpowder; he was that near. Grace of God? More likely the grace of a blank.' She huffed. 'And ain't blanks funny things for an anarchist to load his gun with? And Danny knew that's what they were, and that's why he did it. But he had to, didn't he? The German Ambassador was looking, and he was trying to shut me up, to prevent them finding out who I really was—his sister. He was looking out for me, Mr Holmes, trying to keep me safe; I know that now. I'm surprised my *death's* not been reported in the newspapers!'

'Something of the sort was considered,' Mycroft Holmes said.

'You're no traitor, Mr Holmes, neither is Danny, so I don't understand why you're giving the Germans secret plans,' Mary said. 'Mr Boots wanted to sell the plans to anyone who'd pay. Anyone would do, as far as he was concerned. But Danny insisted they went to the Germans. It had to be them. That didn't make sense to me. Nor, for that matter, does what happens with Danny now.'

Mycroft Holmes arose quietly. He walked to the window and gazed out in silent contemplation. He said nothing for a full minute and a hush filled the room. Then he turned.

'Sherlock said you were clever,' Mycroft Holmes complimented her. 'That little trick at the Seven Dials.' He gave a small laugh. 'He was not exaggerating. Speculate, Miss Finch. You clearly have a brain. Speculate. Why should anyone want to hand over secret plans to their enemy. If indeed Germany is an enemy?'

'Is this a test?' Mary asked.

'Of sorts. But less of you than of us.'

Mary sat upright. She was drumming her fingers against her legs. She had been doing that for the last while, but did not notice.

'Because the plans aren't real,' she said, quickly.

'Oh! Come, come, Miss Finch.' Mr Holmes sighed in annoyance. 'Do not disappoint. You can do better.'

'Someone with rudimentary knowledge of such things would know immediately they were false,' Major Carshaw said drily, 'and suspect a motive.'

Mary closed her eyes and clenched her teeth in annoyance. She'd spoken without thinking the first thing that came to mind. This time, she sat back and thought for a minute.

'Because they are real, but flawed in some aspect that is difficult to spot,' she said, 'at least by someone like Danny, who wouldn't be expected to know otherwise. Or because there's a better torpedo in the navy,' Mary saw Major Carshaw's eyes flick, 'and anything in the plans is of no great loss or consequence.'

Mycroft Holmes nodded as if to himself, but said nothing.

'Was Mr Rentham privy to your plans, Mr Holmes?' Mary asked.

'What do you think?' he asked.

'I think not.' Mary remembered how shocked the Industrialist looked, seated in his office in Dunchester Hall.

'Money is not everything. It is something Fairchild Rentham needs to learn… but, I suspect, he will not.'

Major Carshaw looked at his watch. 'Mr Holmes, the time,' he said.

'Miss Finch,' Mycroft Holmes said, 'come, take a drive with me. It is only to Westminster Bridge.'

'Is this wise, sir?' asked the Major.

'Wise?' Mycroft Holmes mused. 'Under the circumstances, I think it is essential. Come, child, and we will speak of Cassandra.'

❧ 32 ❧

ON WESTMINSTER BRIDGE

THEY CLIMBED aboard a four-wheeler and set out. Archie sat beside Mary, facing Mr Holmes and the Major.

'Of course, things improve,' Mr Holmes said. 'That is the nature of things. What is new today becomes old tomorrow. The cost of a torpedo is slight compared to that of a battleship. Yet one of those little things can embarrass one of those big things, and as such will be worth its weight in gold. And if someone chooses to spend an awful lot of money and invest an awful amount of time and effort into discovering how out-of-date something is; and if they should then choose to believe that what they have in their possession is the best we can do, why should we stop them?'

'Mr Holmes!' Major Carshaw said.

'Yes, yes, Major. I understand your concerns. But

think cardigans.' He smiled at Archie, who looked at him, puzzled.

'But why?' Mary said.

'Cassandra was a prophetess, Miss Finch,' he continued. 'Her curse was to utter true prophesies, but never to be believed. There is going to be a war, Miss Finch. Give it fifteen years, more likely twenty, but a war there will be—another Franco-Prussian affair in which we will become entangled. There is another who believes the same as I. Sadly, he is no longer the German Kaiser's guiding light. So, it is best we plan for it now rather than later. A bird in the hand, Miss Finch. Make plans for what we know and speculate for what we don't.'

'How can you be so sure? I mean, ain't the Kaiser the Queen's grandson?'

'And families do not go to war, I suppose? Did you know, Miss Finch, most murders are committed by people who know each other? There is a new *Great Game* in progress. It is not to be found in Afghanistan or the Indian frontiers, but here in Europe, in places like Whitehall and some dark back rooms in Berlin. Oh, a war there will be. Ambition and jealousy are potent things. I may not live to see the disaster that is coming, I fear you and your young friend will. But coming it is. And when it arrives, it will spare no one its tragedy.

'So we must do what we can. We can only but delay its coming and pray we are wrong, while prudently preparing for the challenges it will bring.' He looked out of the window at the street and gently shook his head, musing quietly, 'Daniel passing you the locket that night at Rentham's was a stupid thing to do. It got you involved. But perhaps there is such a thing as coincidence after all.' He continued to gaze steadily out of the window.

Mary noticed how grim and pained his face became. For once, he seemed aged and burdened by his great brain. He was some master chess player who could foresee many, many moves ahead, and what he saw led inexorably to a disaster.

As the grandmaster he was, his planning must have started years ago, when he first discovered Danny Finch and drew him into his scheme. He made him out to be a murderer and an anarchist, made his criminality seem real so he could infiltrate the enemy, become a double agent, a thing she once called a false friend. But conversely, Mary knew, those things would keep Danny safe.

She sat back and looked up at the roof of the carriage. Her thoughts played through the events of the past few days and she sighed. She understood much now. This *Great Game* was something her brother was playing, and a burden weighed on her to play it with him. He tried to spare her that responsibility by telling her as little as possible. But her mind was far too active for him to succeed, as was her desire to protect him. She wondered what would happen now, and then raised her eyes as if to say *of course*.

She looked at the Major. 'The *Prinz Wilhelm*,' she whispered.

'Excuse me?' Major Carshaw asked.

'It is how Danny will leave the country,' she said. 'He obviously can't stay in England, not with a price on his head. No doubt the ports have his description, and the fishing villages will have been alerted. But who's going to dare check a German gunboat? The *Wilhelm* sails today, doesn't it?'

Major Carshaw gave her a curious and surprised look.

Mycroft Holmes laughed. 'Maybe you should employ Miss Finch, Major. You could do worse. You do not disappoint, Miss Finch. Indeed, you do not.'

The remainder of the journey passed in silence. It was a pleasant ride. The streets around Westminster were busy. After the rain of the last few days, the skies cleared and the weather was warming up. As they passed the Houses of Parliament, Big Ben struck the hour and the carriage came to a halt on the bridge.

'We are here,' Mycroft Holmes said; wearily, she thought. 'I have always thought the view to Charing Cross very good from here. If you would be so kind, Mary, the Major needs to speak to young Archie for a few minutes, and I must attend to business at the other end of the bridge. I will return shortly.'

Mary walked quietly to the side of the bridge as

Mycroft's carriage pulled away, while Archie spoke to the Major. She glanced both ways along the pavement. Silent folks were crossing the road, probably going home from work. Below her, the slow current of the Thames moved sluggishly towards the sea. The sombre brown waters lapped lazily against the stonework of the bridge; the arches sank into the murky depths. Small crafts populated the surface, moving deftly along, casting long shadows as the sun dipped low in the western sky behind the clock tower of Big Ben. A train was moving slowly along the railway bridge by Charing Cross. In the still air, the smoke from the stack rose peacefully to hang above the snaking carriages, and the clacking of the wheels beat a slow, plaintive rhythm. More folks were heading south than north, she thought.

Soon, Big Ben chimed the quarter. More people crossed the bridge. Men in bowler hats with rolled-up umbrellas. A tramp shuffled along. Some children rushed playfully past her; a dour nanny pushed a black perambulator. She saw Mr Holmes's carriage returning. The shadows lengthened across the water and the day was coming to an end.

'Spare a few coppers, miss?' a hoarse voice spoke. The tramp was holding out his hand towards her. He then leant on the railings and a familiar voice said, 'Looks bad, don't it, Midge?'

Mary's heart jumped.

'Danny,' she whispered and a wide grin filled her

face. Even though he was in disguise, she recognised his cheeky smile as he reached out and took her hand.

'Danny… I-I…' Mary stuttered. Her words stuck in her throat and she could hardly breathe, let alone speak. She glanced nervously around. Mr Holmes was sitting alone in the carriage, his eyes towards the Houses of Parliament. Major Carshaw wandered idly with his gaze fixed to the ground, tapping the tip of his umbrella rhythmically. And Archie was leaning against the carriage, kicking his heels.

Below them came a sharp hoot of a steam whistle from the north bank.

'Listen, Midge,' Danny said. 'There ain't much time. I've got so much to say and I'll never manage it all. Mr Holmes tells me you're a clever girl and, if left to yourself, you'll soon figure out what's what. I wish we could speak longer, but they're waiting for me.' He flicked his head towards steps leading down to the water where a small steam launch floated. 'I'm gonna be gone for a long while, Midge, years probably. I wish I could tell you where I'm going and what I'm doing, but I can't for both of our sakes.'

'Germany,' Mary said.

He glanced over; a twinkle lit his eyes.

'No flies on you, is there?'

'Is it dangerous?' Mary asked.

He blew out his breath and gave her hand a squeeze.

'Mum would be proud of you,' he said. 'Dad would

have said you had her looks, but his brains, and then laughed. He wouldn't be half right, as well. Though Mum was a pretty clever woman.'

'Can't I come? Please, Danny, I could—'

He shook his head quietly.

'You can't. Now listen. I ain't doing this for free.' He winked. 'When I found out it was you at Rentham's party, I left instructions with Mr Holmes. We had to do it quickly, but a good portion of my salary is to be paid into an account in your name. Well, I can hardly spend it where I'm going. As long as I'm away, it'll be paid in every New Year. It's yours when you turn seventeen. By then, it'll be worth over two hundred quid. With interest, a lot more. It'll make you an independent woman, and I'm sure you'll make a fine job of that.'

'But, Danny, I don't want... I mean it's—'

'Midge, please, this is hard. I ain't done a good job as a big brother, and this is the least I can do. I missed you so much when they said you were dead, and to find you again... well, it's just... I can't begin to explain. But what I'm doing is important, as I'm sure Mr Holmes has told you. So, find some way to forgive him.' Danny took a deep breath. 'Now, do me a favour. Take this and get it fixed.'

He handed her the half of the locket he tore from her neck that night at Rentham's party when he exchanged it for his.

'There's a jeweller in Bond Street, Mr Holmes knows

who I mean. Get him to make it whole again and wear it for me, will you? We're a family again. Only I'm on holiday and won't be back for a while, is all,' he joked. 'Now, another thing. If you need help, go to Mr Holmes or his brother, or if you can't, then go to the jeweller. Tell him you've a message for Mercury; he'll know what you mean.'

'And the Painter, Mr Quicksilver?' she asked with a smile. Daniel turned his head slowly and nodded approvingly.

'I ain't been called that in a while. The coppers will pick up Mr Boots soon enough, I'm sure. He's hiding in Soho and that's where they're searching.'

Once again, the whistle blew long and hard.

'Duty calls, Midge. Queen Vic commands and we obey,' he said. 'Remember, Danny Fuller is the traitor everyone wants, not Daniel Finch. Now, no tears. Promise?' He squeezed her hand again and walked away.

Mary gazed down the river. She wanted to run after him. Her feet tingled with the expectation of doing so. But she knew she could not. Soon, she saw him descend the steps and climb into the steam launch. It cast off and moved serenely along and down the Thames, cutting through the water and leaving a white wake. He did not look back.

33

A FIGURE IN THE DARK

MARY SNIFFED HER TEARS AWAY. She watched quietly until the launch vanished.

'May I give you a lift to Holland Park?' Mycroft Holmes asked and held open the carriage door. Mary shook her head.

'I'll walk a bit, if it's all right with you, Mr Holmes,' she said. 'I've got things to consider.'

'I make no apology for my actions, Miss Finch,' he said.

'Yet you brought me here so that I could say goodbye.' She knew Mycroft Holmes did so on the spur of the moment and gave him a smile of gratitude. No doubt, it was Danny he was speaking to at the other end of the bridge.

'Then these are yours.' He handed her a small flat

case. 'You will find things of importance within. Some documents, birth certificates and the like, and some small items belonging to your parents. Daniel wanted you to have them. And a bank account book belonging to you. Come, Archibald Socrates Dibble,' Mr Holmes said, loudly. 'I suspect Miss Finch wishes to be alone and I have a hankering for a portion of your Grandmother's pork pie. Do you think she will still be serving at this late an hour? Major Carshaw, did I say how good it is? I believe I did.'

In the gathering gloom of the evening, Mary walked slowly and quietly, her head looking down at the pavement. She decided she would go first to the Dibbles, and then home to Mrs Grady in Holland Park. It had been a long few days since Fairchild Rentham's party. Since then, much had happened that made her both happy and sad at the same time.

Meeting Daniel had been a reunion of sorts, she considered. But she wished it could have been longer. Daniel's *holiday* was indefinite, and she worried that it might be permanent. It was dangerous business, his work.

Before long, Daniel would be aboard the *Prinz Wilhelm* and it would take him to Germany. The hue and cry for the arrest of Danny Fuller would lend credence to his new employer's opinion of him, and Daniel would take the opportunity to ingratiate himself further with them. He would become a spy, a double agent. She shivered, remembering Grandpa Dibble saying how spies got tortured and executed if they were caught. What secrets had Mr Holmes sent Danny to steal? How would he get them back to him? It was a world she did not know existed until recently.

Mr Holmes said he would not apologise for what he'd done. Perhaps it was necessary to keep Daniel safe. Making him out to be a desperate criminal was a ploy, a way to shield him, and now Daniel had to play the part to perfection if he was to remain safe. But even so, she could not yet bring herself to forgive Mr Holmes. She had been denied a brother, and Danny a sister. But at least she understood.

Once she reached Trafalgar Square, Mary found a spot under a light and sat quietly. She opened the case she had been given. It contained her birth certificate and some photographs of her family in happier times. She traced her finger across their faces, but her memory was vague and indistinct. She was only three when they died.

Amongst the items was a parcel of letters. They were correspondence between her mother and father when they were courting. She placed them back; she would read them when she was at home and comfortable in bed with Oscar beside her. Also, within the case were small items of jewellery, some rings and a necklace, and a book of poetry. It was inscribed by her father as a gift to his wife. Pressed flowers lay between several pages.

She found the account book and glanced at it. Already, the account contained fifty pounds. It would contain much more when she turned seventeen in just over three years' time. She could become independent of Mrs Grady, more so if she found a job that paid better. She saw such jobs advertised: type-writers and secretaries; shop girls. The big hotels and the department stores always wanted good, reliable staff. Even though she had no qualifications, she could read, she could write. She was clever and resourceful, wasn't that what both Mr Holmes and Mrs Grady said? And she could learn.

She sat for some more minutes, then arose and made her way down Charing Cross Road and into Leicester Square, and then into Soho heading towards Oxford Street. Curiously, she did not feel the least bit tired, despite her recent ordeal.

Maybe she could become a Detective. It was a pleasant thought. A female Detective. But surely people would only ever ask her to find missing cats and dogs. But that didn't matter. *Lady Mary Finch, Pet Detective with offices in Baker Street.* She grinned broadly.

Lady Mary Finch clutches her royal passport. The dastardly Kaiser of Germany, Queen Victoria's grandson, has abducted her favourite hound, Montgomery. Only she, the intrepid lady Detective, can be trusted to retrieve it and not be the cause of a diplomatic incident that would resound in the corridors of Whitehall and Berlin. She has been chosen over the likes of such masters as

Sherlock Holmes–

Mary burst out laughing, then caught her breath when she saw the faces of the passers-by looking at the strange girl who laughed aloud for no apparent reason. Her face went red and she took to her heels in embarrassment and ran, still laughing, down Greek Street.

'Bloody stupid girl,' a woman said as she passed her.

'Yes, missus, of course, missus,' Mary giggled.

'Is it your birthday?' a man shouted from across the road.

'Birthday and Christmas, mister,' she shouted back.

'Then watch the coppers don't nick you up for being happy,' he joked.

'Only if they can catch me. Tell them they can come and arrest Lady Mary Finch of Holland Park.'

She ran along and turned into an empty street. This wasn't a time for sadness. She had hope. She trusted her brother to be safe, and that one day they would be together again. He was resourceful, of that she had little doubt. And she was the great Lady Mary Finch, someone with a future that she could shape and make successful. She felt like shouting with joy.

'Damn you, Finch!' came a yell from behind her. 'Damn you to hell!'

The next moment, someone struck her hard in the side and she doubled up in pain. She was pushed and tumbled wildly into the mouth of a dimly lit alley. Scrambling to her knees, gasping for the breath that had been knocked from her, Mary fell back against the wall and to the ground as a dark figure advanced towards her. Something metallic glinted in its hand.

'Boots,' Mary choked in horror.

✤ 34 ✤

MARY FINCH, MR BOOTS AND
KITTY SHORT-PANTS

'I SHOULD HAVE DONE for you when you and your friend
pinched Grimwig's jewels,' Boots sneered. 'Then I'd
have been rid of you once and for all.' Dirty, unshaven
and dishevelled, he scowled bitterly. He shook in anger
as he spat at her, 'You and your brother's done me up
good and proper. Ruined me! That's what you've done.'

Mary struggled to her feet. Leaning a hand against the
wall to steady herself, she took a step back. She swallowed whole the rising panic that threatened to cloud her
mind. An icy hand gripped her heart and twisted her
stomach into knots. She shivered, still trying to find her
breath.

Boots advanced slowly and Mary retreated several
steps. Her eyes fixed on his and she saw his utter hatred
for her in the frightful stare he returned.

'But I ain't done yet,' the Butler cursed. 'I'll see you in hell if it's the last thing I do.'

Mary looked around for something she could use as a weapon. There was nothing. She wanted to run, but her legs wobbled and refused to move more than a shuffle. Clutching at the wall, hardening her will, Mary balled her fist. She set her mouth firm, determined to fight to the very end if need be. She remembered what Archie said: '*If you have to fight, strike hard and strike low.*'

'Then I'll do for that brother of yours.' Boots laughed. 'Thinks he can cheat me? Thinks he can hide? I'll find him and tell him just how I killed his sister.'

A vicious sneer cut his dark, angry face. He raised the knife higher and came forward a stride. Mary bent her knees, braced herself and gritted her teeth. The Butler took one more step and shut out the light.

To Mary's utter surprise, there was a sharp crack and Boots yelled in pain. He spun around, dropping the knife. Hopping on one leg, he clutched his knee and Mary heard another sharp crack and Boots's pained howl. He staggered out of the alley, swinging his fists and cursing, only to fall headlong on to the pavement.

Kitty was standing over him. The small girl gave him a stare as bitter as lye, and grimaced. She was holding a cricket stump, and as she lifted it high, she yelled, 'This is for walloping my brother Freddie and giving him a thick ear,' and she struck him. 'And you can keep your ha'penny, we don't want it,' she growled. 'We wouldn't touch it with a bargepole, even if you begged us to take it.'

A small crowd was gathering as she raised the stump once more. Mr Boots curled into a ball and his hands shot around to protect his head.

'And this is for Mary…' Kitty was about to hit him again when the stump was yanked out of her hand. Constable O'Connor grabbed the fierce little girl and lifted her, kicking, spitting and screaming, into the air and away.

'All right, all right, enough,' he shouted. 'He's had enough. He's down and ain't getting up.'

'Let me at him.' Kitty fought and scratched like a tiger against the policeman's iron grip.

'Will you shut it?' O'Connor shouted and sat the girl down heavily in the street. 'Can't you see? Mary needs help and I can't deal with you both.'

O'Connor rushed over to Mary, leaving Boots where he lay, moaning and holding his knee. Carefully, he helped Mary out from the alley and told her to sit. Removing her hand from where she clutched her side, he checked the injury. A nasty bruise was quickly developing. She winced in pain, but her ribs were intact and she was all right; only a little the worse for wear with the cuts on her head and her knee.

He nodded. 'You've been in the wars.' He grinned and winked. 'But I've seen worse at a vicar's tea party.'

Mary's heart was still pounding; she was sweating

profusely and trembling, but a gasp of utter relief left her lips. She sat with her back against the lamppost, suddenly weary. The crowd had grown by the time Inspector Gregson came running up. The Inspector stood above Boots with his hands on his hips, nodding his head to the policeman with approval.

'Well done, O'Connor,' he said. 'It's another of them anarchists we were told to look out for. Cameron Boots, we've got you now. Just your bomber friend to find and we'll have you all. You'll get your stripes back in no time at this rate, O'Connor.'

'I didn't catch him, sir,' O'Connor said. 'She did.'

He stepped across to reveal the small girl. Instantly, the smile left Inspector Gregson's face and vanished completely from Kitty's.

'Kitty Short-Pants!' he growled.

'Mr Gregson!' Kitty's startled eyes bulged wide. In the space of a heartbeat, Kitty spun around and was charging headlong down the street, hair flying, clothes flapping, elbows pumping.

'Get her,' Gregson bellowed. 'Don't stand there. Get her,' and O'Connor took up the chase. But Mary had a distinct impression that O'Connor was dawdling. When he'd chased her one winter's evening, he'd easily caught her, and her legs were a good deal longer than those of Kitty Short-Pants. She doubted he would catch the small girl. She was grateful that Kitty was there to help, though what accident of fate brought her there, she did not know.

When O'Connor returned from his unsuccessful chase, putting on a show by puffing and panting, Mary whispered to him.

'*Sargent,* surely there must be a reward for Boots by now?'

O'Conner winked, 'Just issued. I'll see the young lady gets it. Twenty-five quid, I think it is."

'And a pardon?' Mary winked back. 'After all, Mr Gregson can't very well arrest a hero, can he?'

<hr>

Mary was taken to Bow Street police station, where the police surgeon checked that she had no other injuries. Afterwards, a hansom took her to Holland Park. Mrs Grady sent her to bed immediately, despite Mary's complaints that she was fine. In truth, she felt embarrassed that everyone was fussing over her.

Cook made soup and Mr Venables, brought it up to her room. For a while, they, along with Mrs Grady and Ella and Fortune, sat with her and she told them what happened. When they all left, she was finally alone with Oscar, the mouser.

The cat climbed on to her bed, a mournful look in his eyes. Or was it one of relief that everyone left and he could find some peace? He tucked in beside Mary and drew his tail around his nose and fell asleep. Mary stroked the silky fur and sat back.

With Boots in custody, Danny would be safer. He would vanish, she had no doubt of that if Major Carshaw had a say in things, and be lost in some prison for many, many years to come.

Tomorrow was a new day, and for reasons she could not explain, Mary felt as if it would be the first day of her life. When she'd initially met Mrs Grady, she'd told her she had plans to better herself. Somehow, it felt as if the time was right to realise them.

Mary opened the case that Mycroft Holmes had given her and took out the bundle of letters. She chose one.

'*My Dearest, Abbie…*'

AUTHOR'S NOTES

At the beginning of the book, Mrs Grady describes anarchists as, *'Nasty people who want to overthrow the government. They believe wealth should be distributed evenly. They want to abolish the state – that is, the government – as they believe it to be harmful and irrelevant. So, they plant bombs and blow things and people up.'*

Of course, this is an oversimplification. In late Victorian England, when the book is set, and indeed, around the world at that time, anarchists made the news for their violent tendencies and they were greatly feared. People believed that they wanted revolution, and the storyline of the book plays on those fears.

Queen Victoria was related to many of the great royal houses of Europe. The German Kaiser, Wilhelm II, was her eldest grandchild; Nicholas II, Czar of Russia, was married to Victoria's favourite granddaughter, Alix of Hesse. During Queen Victoria's reign, Britain was the *superpower* of the age. However, in the period the book is set, there began a rivalry between Britain and Germany. This would encompass overseas territories, industrial progress and military advances. Some of this would lead to the First World War that Mycroft Holmes fears is coming.

The rivalry between Germany and Britain would become a fierce one, but the *Great Game* was a political and diplomatic rivalry between the British and Russian Empires over Afghanistan, Tibet and neighbouring countries. Beginning in the 1830s, Britain wanted to gain control of the Emirate of Afghanistan to protect her interest in India from Russian influence in the region. It was the cause of numerous wars, many of them failed conflicts. It was considered officially ended in 1895, some two years after our story. Rudyard Kipling's book, *Kim,* (1901) popularised the term *Great Game* and introduced to us the idea of great power rivalry.

Lastly, a note on the London Underground, where Mary finds herself in danger from Mr Boots. On 10 January 1863, the Metropolitan Railway opened the world's first underground railway. It was an immediate success, carrying an amazing 38,000 passengers on the opening day! The line ran between Paddington (which was called Bishop's Road at the time) and Farringdon, using wooden carriages hauled by steam locomotives: a sooty, smoky affair. Electrification would not happen fully until the turn of the new century.

Baker Street was one of the stations on the line, and many lines and stations would be added soon after. Originally, passengers had the choice of travelling either in a first-class compartment (the most expensive and luxurious), or in second- or third-class compartments. Lighting was provided by gas – there were two gas lights in first class, and one each in second- and third-class compartments.

If you travel on the underground Circle Line to Baker Street, you can still see the magnificent Victorian architecture and the wonderful arched ceiling.

ACKNOWLEDGMENTS

Thank you to all who have contributed to the writing of this book. There have been many patiently reading and commenting on sections, listening and offering good advice.

REVIEW REQUEST

If you have enjoyed reading this book, please leave a
review on Amazon, Goodreads or BookBub.
Every single review help new readers discover my books.

For more information you can visit my website:
https://saywackwrites.com

or contact me by email:
saywackwrites@gmail.com

or come and say Hi! on my facebook page:
https://www.facebook.com/SSSaywack